Praise for The Helios Disaster

"The emotional intensity created by Boström Knausgård recalls Sylvia Plath, but her spare, accelerating modern myth owes something to the poet/classicist Anne Carson's novels in verse. This novella cannot be read quickly, its psychological range and febrile prose demand attentiveness. It takes skill and imagination to describe extreme emotions in ways to which everybody can relate but that's what Boström Knausgård achieves in this short, piercing book."

The Independent

"The story is tightly, cleverly organized around a central idea: to show how Anna's perceptive, disturbed mind struggles to impose some kind of mental order and, finally, fails. The author's passionate involvement with her protagonist illuminates what it is like to slide irresistibly away from reality."

Swedish Book Review

"Linda Boström Knausgård's style is magical, hallucinatory, and very poetic. Passionate, refined, and as clear as cool water."

Aftonbladet

"*The Helios Disaster* is a story about longing for a father and about prepubescence. About the will to die, refusal, and a sun shining far too brightly. But in this field of tension there is also a simple happiness. Boström Knausgård's authorship keeps getting better and better."
Dagens Nyheter

"It is simple and it is grand, a story about a girl who came too close to the sun. *The Helios Disaster* shines!"
Kulturnytt i P1, Sveriges Radio (Swedish Public Radio)

"*The Helios Disaster* is an insightful story about mental illness and missing a father. Linda Boström Knausgård manages to fill the rather monotonous hospital existence with a tension so powerful and poetic that one is actually quite taken by it and reads it without missing a single detail."
Kulturnyheterna SVT

"*The Helios Disaster* is a dense, tender, painful novel written in a prose which, always poetic, touches, shakes, and makes a mess."
Helsingborgs Dagblad

"Chosen for the unsentimental language of her portrayal of human existence on the border between a world distorted by psychosis and reality's structured existence. Her stories are written according to the logic of myths, never asking why, but allowing an understanding of ourselves that is difficult to be determined in the dominant categories."

JURY, MARE KANDRE PRIZE

Praise for Welcome to America

"Here, restraint and ambiguity prevail, whether it's about the intensity of the abuse Ellen sustained or the veracity of her assertions. Regardless, it's a taut portrait of how difficult it can be to reconcile ideals about faith and family with their messier realities. An intense, recursive book that evokes the chill despair of a Bergman film."
Kirkus Reviews

"Knausgaard is an impressive writer, who has created a unique, powerful lead in a world all her own."
Publishers Weekly

"Every word is there for a reason."
Minn Post

"A singular and thought-provoking story with a child narrator you won't soon forget."
Book Riot

"Knausgård's story of a family in crisis is shocking and imaginative. Everything is written in beautiful and sparse prose which suggests that, after all, from darkness comes light."
JURY, AUGUST PRIZE

"Knausgård's artistry is masterful."
Bookslut

"*Welcome to America* presents itself as an étude in the musical sense of the term: a basic theme that varies to infinity, acquiring with each new variation a new unprecedented facet. A triumph."
Le Monde

"The incandescent Welcome to America allows one to discover the author's vibrant and powerful universe."
Lire

"Gets you in the gut. A delirious dance."
L'Alsace Quotidien

"A tender novel about a mute girl: gentle, sensitive, minimal, concise, subtle, and brutal. This is writing as self-defense and liberation."
VOLKER WEIDERMANN, *Spiegel*

THE HELIOS DISASTER

LINDA BOSTRÖM KNAUSGÅRD

THE HELIOS DISASTER

Translated from the Swedish
by Rachel Willson-Broyles

WORLD EDITIONS
New York, London, Amsterdam

Published in the USA in 2020 by World Editions LLC, New York
Published in the UK in 2015 by World Editions Ltd., London

World Editions
New York/London/Amsterdam

Copyright © Linda Boström Knausgård, 2013
English translation copyright © Rachel Willson-Broyles, 2015
Cover image © Paul Citroen / Nederlands Fotomuseum
Author portrait © Christina Ottosson Öygarden

Printed by Lake Book, USA

This book is a work of fiction. Any resemblance to actual persons, living or dead, or actual events is purely coincidental. The opinions expressed therein are those of the characters and should not be confused with those of the author.

Library of Congress Cataloging in Publication Data is available

ISBN 978-1-64286-068-9

First published as *Helioskatastrofen* in Sweden in 2013 by Modernista, by arrangement with Nilsson Literary Agency, Sweden

The cost of this translation was defrayed by a subsidy from the Swedish Arts Council, gratefully acknowledged.

All rights reserved. No part of this publication may be reproduced, stored in or introduced into a retrieval system, or transmitted, in any form, or by any means (electronic, mechanical, photocopying, recording or otherwise) without the prior written permission of the publisher.

Twitter: @WorldEdBooks
Facebook: @WorldEditionsInternationalPublishing
Instagram: @WorldEdBooks
www.worldeditions.org

Book Club Discussion Guides are available on our website.

PART ONE

I AM BORN of a father. I split his head. For an instant that is as long as life itself we face one another and look each other in the eye. You are my father, I tell him with my eyes. My father. The person in front of me, standing in the blood on the floor, is my father. His woollen socks suck it up greedily and turn red. The blood sinks into the worn wooden floor and I think, *his eyes are green like mine.*

How, at my birth, do I know that? That my eyes are green like the sea.

He looks at me. At my shining armour. He lifts his hand. Touches my cheek with it. And I lift my hand and close it around his. Lean against him. His arms, which embrace me. We cry together. Warm, salty tears and snot run down my face. I want nothing but to stand like this with my father and feel his warmth, listen to the beating of his heart. I have a father. I am my father's daughter. These words ring through me like bells in that instant.

Then he screams.

His scream tears everything apart. I will never again be close to him. Never again rest my head against his chest. We have met and must immediately part. He could do no more than give me life. The scream presses my lips together; they want to shout at him to stop. *You're scaring me*, grows within my mouth. My temples ache. All the love turns to rage in my chest.

So much screaming, I think, and I immediately want to plunge my lance into his heart to make it stop. I'm afraid. Just a child.

He doesn't stop screaming. He holds his

head. Presses his strong hands to it as if to close what has opened.

*

I take off my armour and hide my lance in the kitchen bench. I am wearing my helmet when I go out into the world for the first time. I am twelve years old when I show up in the village in the north.

I step into the snow with bare feet. I don't get far. A naked girl with a golden helmet on her head. Moreover, there are many people who saw the ambulance that picked up my father after the neighbour couple came running to find out what had happened. They had heard his scream from far away. And the neighbours who saw me in the armour on the floor in my father's living room wanted to know. Had I been kept hidden? Who was I? A child whom no one had seen. Where were my parents?

It was chaos. What should I say?

'My name is Greta,' said the neighbour lady. 'Who are you?'

I didn't answer. My tongue suddenly felt large and shapeless, thick and in the way.

'You have to put something on.'

She took off her down coat and put it around me. She carefully but firmly took me by the elbow and led me to their house, which was on the same street as my father's. She led me like this, into the warm, as they apparently say, and into the kitchen, where she sat me down on a chair.

What do I do now? My thoughts were jumbled around and I longed for my father's eyes. Instead I got warm milk with honey and cinnamon, and clothes.

'I'll help you,' she said when she saw that I only stared at the clothes.

'Dear girl. Here are some underpants, there we go. First one foot, then the other. Good. Long johns. They're made of wool, so you won't freeze. It's cold up here right now, you know. It's over twenty below freezing. Then the undershirt. You can have these clothes. They're too small for me now.' She dressed me from head to toe. Pants and knitwear and everything. I also received a coat, and a hat and mittens. I thought of the armour in the kitchen bench and wanted to go there.

'Now you have to tell me who you are,' Greta said when I had drunk the milk and eaten up the reindeer-meat sandwich. *Reindeer meat*, I thought, storing the words in my memory. That salty and bloody taste.

'I want to go to my father,' I said.

'Dear child. Conrad doesn't have any children.'

'He has me,' I said, getting up from the chair.

Greta looked at me gravely.

'Has he been mean to you? Conrad is a bit different, after all.'

'No.'

Would a father be mean to his child? To his own child?

'Has he kept you hidden?'

Greta was kind. I understood this, even if what I wanted most of all was to knock the chair I was sitting on to pieces and destroy the house after what she'd said about my father. *She doesn't know any better*; the thought that came to me calmed me down and I realized two things: that no one would ever understand how I came to be in Conrad's kitchen and that I would therefore be alone for the rest of my life.

Greta drove me to the social-services office in the city. She had made a call, and I had heard the words: 'Girl. Conrad. I don't know what to do. I can't keep the girl here.' And then this: 'If I didn't know better, I would believe that a miracle has happened.' Miracle. That was the word that stuck, and I didn't know where to put the word, so I looked at Greta to keep more words from coming out of her.

My father had acute schizophrenia and was sent, screaming, to the mental hospital in Skellefteå, where his story was disregarded and his headache was alleviated with medicine so strong that, in the end, he himself was sceptical that it had really happened. But I didn't know that then, as I sat in Greta's car looking at all the white. I still believed that I would live in the house with the dirty rag rugs and the unwashed windows. That Conrad would come back and that we would be father and daughter, as it had been decided in that instant when everything between us was still good.

*

Snow. Snow. I learned the word right away. Understood that it was important. It was the only thing I could see besides the road and Greta.

'The reindeer are having a hard time this year. The Sami are driving them further and further down to find pasture, but the snow line is all the way down to Stockholm. And it's only fall. Just think. So much snow and it's only October.'

October, I thought. *Reindeer. Sami*, I thought, and I saw a flowing body of water pushing its way out of the landscape.

'The river,' said Greta. 'Do you know what I'm talking about?'

I shook my head. The river. The river.

'We'll be in the city in an hour. They're going to ask questions. Do you know what I mean?'

I looked out the window. The river rushed

along as if it were playing. It hopped and twisted. I rested my forehead against the window and it was like it was singing, the river.

The helmet was beside me in the back seat. I stroked it with my hand, and the fact that it was there calmed me.

'People are going to talk, you know. A naked girl in Conrad's house.'

'He is my father. I don't know the rest,' I said.

'No,' said Greta, and she concentrated on driving.

There was an ache within my chest, and I looked out across the snow that lay on the branches of the trees, on the fields and the meadows. *It is sadness*, I said to the snow. *That's what is hurting and pushing out the tears. What will I do? I don't know anything about my future. Who am I?* I asked the snow.

The city grew closer. Wooden houses, several storeys high. The people walking on the street looked like black birds against all the white. They flocked together and glided away from each other. *They know nothing,* I thought, and then: *Is this where I belong? Among them? We have nothing to do with one another.* It was clear as they rushed along. That we wouldn't become familiar with one another. I closed my eyes and remembered Conrad's eyes. Those calm eyes looking at me.

*

I was placed in a home. The family I was going to live with had always wanted a girl. They already had two boys as it was.

The social-services lady was called Birgit, and there wasn't much to her. We didn't say much to each other because she smoked the whole time. Cigarettes and smoke were all over the room with the telephone and the lingonberry almanac she was looking at.

'It's a difficult situation, but I'm sure we'll figure something out.'

Her accent was like Greta's, and that was something they had up here. Something in common. As she exhaled the cigarette smoke she said that the best option was probably Birgitta and Sven. Sweet people. They had always wanted to have a girl, and here she gave me an exhortative smile, as if she demanded a smile in return, since she was putting in so much effort on my behalf.

I didn't smile. I didn't speak. I hadn't mentioned my father's name because I could not utter it in this ugly room with the picture and the desk and the lady.

I coughed from the smoke when she asked me if it sounded okay.

'Does that sound okay?' she said.

'Good people. Really normal and nice. Active in club life. Lots of sports. Those things are important when there are so few of us. Sticking together. You understand that, don't you?'

'I'd rather live with Greta,' I finally said.

But that wasn't true. I would go to my father. Get my armour and free him. Nothing else was possible, now that I wanted it so much.

'Greta doesn't want you, you see. But I have to know'—she coughed—'how you got here. Tell me. It will feel better as soon as you tell me.' She paused and took a drag on her cigarette, in and out. 'Even if it's horrible, it will feel better afterward.'

Everything went quiet. I looked out at the white outside the window. All the words she had said struck me. *So many words for nothing*, I thought.

A thought came to me: *The snow is beautiful.* All the white. I thought I could say it. As an experiment.

'The snow is beautiful.'

The social-services lady didn't say anything to that. Instead she said that she helped people who lived under very difficult circumstances.

'Where is he?' I said. 'Where is my father?'

She took a little drag on her cigarette and thought for a long time, it looked like. She ran her index finger across the desk pad.

'You have to have a name.'

She stood up and her skirt swung and twisted around her legs as she walked to the bookcase full of binders and catalogues, and she took one out, a binder with a red spine, and then she sat down and looked at me.

'You look like an Anna,' she said. 'Anna

Bergström. That sounds nice,' she said, looking at me.

Her gaze seemed to get stuck, so I looked out the window again at all the snow that lay there outside like it was waiting for me. That's how it felt. As if it were waiting for me.

I was placed in a home. I should be glad, said the social-services lady. I should be glad, Greta said later, in the waiting room.

'You couldn't have gotten a better family. A family is like a little flock, and they stick together and love each other,' said Greta. 'I'm going to give you a dictionary. Can you read?'

Read. Flock.

I knew I had to get home to my father. That was the only thing I knew. I would find that place and lead him home. I could tempt him with reindeer meat if he wouldn't come on his own, I thought.

I was to wait there and they would come to get me. They had already been contacted. Even if they had probably been picturing a younger girl, they were happy. Birgitta did embroidery for the handicraft lottery. The dad, Sven—it stung me when she said that word, *dad*, even though I had never heard it before—was an art teacher, a real personality in the village.

I cried. The tears were both warm and cold. The warm ones were for my father, whom I would never see again. Was that so? Was that true? I dug deep into myself and asked the question once more: *Would I ever see my father again?*

The cold tears were because I would be cared for after all. The cold tears were for the village and the community lottery. The promise of an evening meal and the two boys they had. Would we like each other?

I realized that I had to grow up. Grow up to be able to visit my father at the hospital.

'You don't want to try one last time to tell me where you come from?' the lady asked, trying to look trustworthy.

'I don't know,' I said.

Greta sat there waiting. She was truly kind. She would have been home by now if she had left on time as she had planned.

'Go into the bathroom and wipe your face,' she said.

I went into a small room, and inside I was drawn to the mirror. My face wasn't foreign, like everything else. I ran the faucet and washed away my tears. Rinsed my hands with the warm water for a long, long time, and the warmth that spread through me did me good and I realized that I had been cold. I never wanted to stop, and finally Greta knocked on the door and I went out. I left the room with the red-and-grey-spotted linoleum floor. I shut the door so hard it echoed.

'Are you angry?' Greta asked.

I sat down on the sofa.

'My name is Anna,' I said.

'That's a good name. Anna. It suits you.'

'Can't you just go?' I said, looking at her. 'I think that's enough of everything anyway. There's nothing in here.'

'Yes,' she said, reaching for her coat. 'Goodbye, my friend, I'm sure things will go well for you.'

'Is this hell?' I asked her suddenly. I don't know where it came from.

She became frightened, I could tell. Was I the one who scared her? But I wanted to know so I shook her arm.

She pulled her arm away.

'No,' she said. 'This isn't hell.'

They picked me up at the social-services office. The dad and the mom and their sons, Urban and Ulf. I didn't dare to look at them, because I thought that they would see in my eyes that I wouldn't stay with them. That they weren't getting me the way they thought. I sat on the red sofa looking down at my hands. I didn't know what I should do with them, so I just looked at them. Maybe that was proper, I thought. They were still bloody, even though I'd washed them. I smelled the blood, which had dried and was dark red in the lines that ran along my hands, and the sweet, slightly burned smell calmed me.

A black exhaustion swooped down on me. I fell over, down into the exhaustion, which was black and red at the edges. I could feel them carrying me, carrying me like a child to the car they had waiting out there. From far off, I felt Birgitta and Sven lay me across Urban's and Ulf's laps in the back seat.

I slept for three days and three nights. When I woke up, I was in a bed and Ulf was sitting next to me and smiling with his face, or with his mouth and eyes, was how he was smiling, and he told me about the doctor who had been there and done tests while I slept, and then he said two things: that I was a real beauty and that I should stick with him.

'You don't know anything, after all, and I know everything. Urban knows a lot too; he has more soul, but he's quieter and stuff and I need a sister who can help me. I have an awful lot to do, you see.'

'Like what?' I asked.

'We'll get to that later. We'll get to all of that later. Remember, you don't know any-thing.'

I thought of the snow and noticed that I became angry. 'Can you take me to the house where my dad lives?'

'All of that is simple,' said Ulf. 'You're

going to help me with the really hard things,' he said.

I fell asleep again. I saw sleep coming and it was like green fingers stretching into my head and on down into my body. I couldn't move. I sank through the mattress and lay under the bed for quite a while, looking into the slatted bottom of the bed and at the dust bunnies, until I got up again and floated up beneath the ceiling. I looked down at Ulf, who was still sitting at my side. I saw myself with closed eyes and I tried to get back down to where I was. Because I could see it, that I was lying there. The green pulled me back and I crashed down into myself like when you dive into the sea.

'I VOW TO do my best to promote the goals of the IOGT as they are written in the principles and programmes. Therewith I pledge to live a sober life; that is, I will not imbibe alcoholic beverages with greater than 2.25 per cent alcohol by volume, nor will I use narcotics, or other poisons with intoxicating effects.'

The entire assembly mumbled this pledge. There were many teetotallers in the village, and people even came from the city and the other villages. Sven stood at the very front, at the wood-coloured podium, looking out over the members who had gathered that Saturday evening to avow sobriety and its benefits. I had grown used to calling Sven 'dad,' because the word 'father' hid inside me like a secret. I was taking care of the coffee things with Birgitta and the boys. Birgitta had been baking buns all day, and Ulf, Urban, and I had run around the village knocking on doors. 'It's time for temperance,' Ulf said, and Urban stood behind him, watching with that expression he had. The one that immediately made you want to do as he wished. I hadn't grown used to this, and I stood farther back, on the street in the snow, watching, but they still wanted me to come along.

'It's more convincing with a girl,' said Ulf, who was the one who did most of the talking.

He was a fast talker, and he could make his eyes and his words glitter, even though he was firm.

We were gathering members for IOGT, and on the same street, the pastor's children were gathering members for the

Pentecostal church. Most people were in both. When people weren't professing faith in sobriety or God, they did sports. I had learned to ski in the tracks in the woods, and it was like flying. Flying, that's what it was like. The snow, the skis, the ski wax, and out in the tracks. One might say that I lived for my skis. That they were my best friends, that we belonged together, and that was clearly how things were between us. It wasn't something I needed to learn, like the vow of temperance, which I mumbled along with but didn't understand while I lined up plastic cups as quietly as possible on the long table with the paper tablecloth.

My father existed somewhere. He lived and breathed there. Did he ever think of me, his daughter? Did he yearn for me?

'Ulf,' I said as quietly as I could, but without whispering. 'Do you know Conrad?'

'No,' he said. 'But I know people who know.'

'Soon I'm going to tell you something important,' he said. 'It has to do with what we're going to do, the two of us. You and me. There's not going to be anyone else, understand?'

'If you help me with Conrad,' I said, 'then I'll do what you want. But it has to happen in that order.'

'The order doesn't matter to me. I'm patient,' Ulf said, placing the pump thermoses on the table. 'You know I go driving at night.'

I did know. Sven hid the car key under his pillow, but he slept so deeply that it didn't matter. Ulf just lifted up the pillow and then it wasn't long before the car started. Where he drove, I didn't know. But after a few hours the car came back. I heard him pulling up. He didn't do anything to avoid being heard, he wasn't careful or anything—in fact, the brakes screeched and I thought he must have been going fast.

Ulf put back the key and went to bed. The only problem was that it was hard to wake him up later in the morning.

'I know who knows,' he said again. 'You know Greta, of course, but we can't ask her, but there's Rolf in the next village.' Ulf put the buns in baskets.

*

No one talked to me except those in the family. Birgitta in particular was worried about me. And she must have been disappointed, too. She had wanted her own girl, who could be like her. Just like her, sitting next to her on the sofa after dinner, doing needlework or just talking. I never talked, or almost never, even though I knew all the words and even though I sounded like everyone else now.

I tried sitting next to her on the curved leather sofa with my teacup, making an effort. I ate the cookies with a good appetite: almond cookies, thumbprint cookies, Finnish shortbread. The crumbs got caught in the corners of my mouth and she frequently wiped them off with a napkin and asked me to be a little more careful.

'Be a little careful with yourself,' she might say. 'We only have one life, and it's important to take care of ourselves, you see. You ought to brush your hair and shower every day. It's important, you see. Just as important as everything else.'

'What is everything else?' I asked.

'That's your emotions. What happens inside you when you're in the world.'

'Like when I'm skiing and the memories come?' I asked.

'Which memories?' she asked. 'What is it you remember?'

Here I thought carefully. Which memory should I give her, so as not to scare her?

'Like my memory of Father,' I tried, even though I knew it was the wrong memory.

'Well, that memory is yours alone,' she said. 'We can never understand that memory. You have to gather up other memories. The ones that are here. Think about your room, for example. About what is there.'

I did as she said. I moved to my room with the bed and the floral duvet cover and the brown roller blinds, the blonde-wood nightstand that Sven had made for me. It was like a little cabinet with a door and a knob, and inside it was the book I read at night before I went to sleep. The book about God I'd received from the social-services lady, like a sort of farewell gift.

'You're a beautiful girl, you know. And

with beauty comes certain privileges.'

Privileges? I thought. And I devoured the word from beginning to end.

'Yes, advantages. It's easy to be liked. Even if you have to make an effort.'

Make an effort, I thought, wiping my mouth with the napkin.

I realized that this conversation was important to her, Birgitta. She wanted to get to know me. But I didn't know how to do that. I didn't want to know.

I walked around and around in the house. Everything was made of blonde wood: the kitchen-cabinet doors, the beds, and the stairs down to the bedrooms and the ping-pong room. The sons had put up stickers all over: 'Orienteers ditch the booze' or 'Skiers ditch the booze.' I had a sticker, too; it was round, on the headboard of my bed: 'Gymnasts ditch the booze,' and I felt like that sticker had been chosen just for me by the sons. I was going to be a gymnast, the sticker seemed to be saying.

The house had been built on a hill, so on one side, toward the street, it was one storey, but in the other direction it was two. It was called a 'daylight basement,' Sven had said. Sven had built the house himself from the ground up. I realized by the way he spoke about it that the house was the most important thing that had happened in his life, and I thought that it was different, what was important. After the hill came the sheep pastures and then it was open all the way to the river that ran through there, and that overflowed in the spring. That's what Urban had said, and that's where he was most of the time, at the river, and he told me about the summers when it dried out and the bottom was visible for several weeks.

Sometimes I got to go with him. We walked together in silence; Urban carried the fishing rods and I had the plastic bag with the thermos of coffee. Urban was fifteen, and he already drank coffee and thought I could learn too, so I drank small sips out of the plastic mug when we took a break. I liked the smell more than the taste, but mostly I liked the warmth, so I drank quick sips so the coffee burned my mouth and numbed the roof of my mouth and my tongue, and then it didn't taste as strong. Urban taught me to cast. Sometimes we fished with flies, but occasionally we had live bait. Urban stood behind me and we held the rod together and it danced with us and in the air until the fly hit the surface of the water. I liked standing so close to Urban and I would lean against him and his patience, which never ran out. Again and again I got to learn how the line would dance. He probably noticed that I pressed against him, but he never let it show. Whether he liked it the way I liked it, or whether he was just letting me have my way.

The water sparkled and the current was strong. We slowly walked along the bank, rods in hand. Following the current and not saying anything for several hours.

He also smoked cigarettes with his coffee. Took a pack out of his pocket and lit one. I looked at him; I was surprised, because I thought about the vow of sobriety and everything else one wasn't allowed to do, but I didn't dare to ask; but he must have seen my look the first time it happened because he said, 'It's for my thoughts. And this thing about intoxicants,' he said then. 'Sven is misinformed. Intoxicants are the best thing ever. You just can't use them too much and you have to choose your timing carefully. And it takes its toll, being drunk. You have to be sure you have plenty of time, both for the drinking itself and for afterwards.'

I didn't dare to ask if I could be there sometime when he was drinking. But I tasted the cigarette he held out. Drew in the smoke and held it in my mouth, before I spit it out.

'You should pull a little down into your lungs, but be careful, starting out. The smoke should go down and fight with your lungs. The battle is what's so nice about it, and the nicotine, or the poison itself, goes right up into your brain, pulling your thoughts straight. You'll like it.'

'Yes, next time I'll do it right,' I said.

Urban had never before spoken to me for so long, and I needed to sit with the words for a long time, turning them over. What was it he had told me?

Did he keep secrets from the family?

'Does Sven know about all of this?' I asked. 'About the smoking, and that you drink?'

'Yes,' he said.

'Does it upset him? Since he believes in sobriety so much?'

'I suppose Dad is upset. But that's nothing to worry about.'

'Where does Ulf drive at night?' I asked him then, because it seemed to be the right moment to ask a question like that.

'To see a girl in the next village,' he said.

Birgitta was going to Umeå to buy new patterns in the needlework store. I was going to go with her, and she dressed me in a loden coat and *Lovikka* mittens. I had received a white fur hat too, and I thought I looked like a little girl when I saw myself in the mirror. Like she probably wanted me to be. The car smelled like gum, because Birgitta was always chewing it. She had her good coat on, and she had curled her hair. She wasn't wearing a hat, even though it was below freezing. She probably wanted to show off her hair. The car ride to the city took forty minutes, and Birgitta listened to music the whole way. I had heard the organ playing in the Pentecostal church, and it was a sound that shook me until tears came. And the pastor, who sang with his deep voice while the choir followed him with their high voices. We would play with the pastor's sons, but they didn't like the church itself, Sven and Birgitta. They had their own beliefs, after all, I thought. But I had kept the music.

Birgitta listened to music from the fifties, she said.

'Back when I was young and went to dances they played these tunes. This music makes me happy, you see?'

I understood that it made her happy, because she sang along with the choruses, really belted them out, and I thought about the way everyone in the family acted different when they were by themselves, or when Sven wasn't there. The snow along the road was dirty. Birgitta let the car race on.

Later, in the store, she asked to see the

new patterns. The woman who owned the store proudly brought out the carton and showed her: a white moose in a forest, fairies dancing in a misty meadow, a wreath of roses that said 'a day of plenty is never blessed, a day of thirst is always best.'

'Which one should I pick?' Birgitta asked.

'The white moose,' I said.

'Then I'll embroider that one for you. And I'll take the wreath of roses for myself,' she said to the lady in the store.

I looked at the pattern with the white moose. Was it going to be mine? Something so beautiful? My eyes burned and I was glad when we left the store and the tears that threatened to fall from my eyes disappeared in the dry air.

'Let's go to the bookstore too,' Birgitta said, taking my arm.

It was clear that she enjoyed being in the city. I didn't know how I should feel. Like a friend or a daughter, but of course I was neither, so I straightened my back and pulled away until she let me walk on my own.

Birgitta was going to buy a new novel in the bookstore.

'I'll take one by our own,' Birgitta said, placing the book on the counter. 'He's just had a new one come out,' she said to me, showing me the book.

'Do you want anything?' she asked me. 'It would be good for you to read,' she said then, looking over at the shelf of children's books.

'That,' I said, pointing at the wall.

'What is it?' Birgitta said, looking at it.

'A map of the Mediterranean,' I said.

The axe split the wood and the pieces fell in opposite directions.

'You don't have to put in any effort at all,' said Urban. 'The weight of the axe is enough; it's just the way you move it that's important. Try again.'

I tried again. Placed the log on the chopping block and held the axe behind my back. This time I just followed the movement and struck the log without putting any strength behind it, and I was surprised when the wood obediently split with only a little thunk.

'There, now you can do it,' Urban said, walking off.

The river was roaring down there as I split one log after another. It forced its way on and seemed to give a relieved sigh as it spread out. The snow hung on the branches and the trees and if you were to walk straight out into it you would sink to your shoulders.

It was its own rhythm, with the axe ringing and the river speaking down there. It was as if my body were caught in motion and I thought it was like music. I chopped and chopped. I would do the whole pile. The sun was red from the sunset. Steam rushed out of my mouth with each breath. *I'm going to write a letter*, I said to myself. *I will start tonight*, I thought, splitting another log. I don't know how long I stood there, but eventually Urban came back.

'Stop now,' he said. 'Come in and have some coffee, at least. Your lips are all blue.'

I didn't notice that I was cold until I came into the house, where the evening coffee and snack were set out on the table.

I took out a pen and paper and sat down at my desk. Stars were shining in the sky. I knew that I just had to start. Nothing was more right than anything else.

'Conrad,' I wrote. 'It's me, writing to you. You remember me. Don't think otherwise. Soon it will be time for us to meet again. I live with a family. Everyone is nice to me. I've learned most things in the last few weeks. I know that you're in the hospital in the city. You have to tell me everything.

Your daughter.'

I sealed the envelope, wrote my address on the back, and paged through the phone book I had taken from the hall table on the top floor.

I found the hospital and wrote the address and Conrad's name. There was probably only one Conrad there. The letter would reach him, I was sure of it.

The mailbox was next to the kiosk beside the grocery store. I put on my down coat and went out in the cold with my letter. The snow crunched and I didn't think about how I was only wearing a nightgown underneath. I didn't notice the cold or the stars as I walked. Each breath was steam. The snow shone in the dark. *Life is so beautiful* came to me and I didn't know if it was a psalm I had heard or if it was just something I thought. *I don't want to die* came to me next, and I didn't know that. That I had wanted to die, but now I realized that it was true.

I had a few coins in my pocket, and they were enough for the stamp. I licked the stamp carefully and pressed it to the letter. The mailbox accepted the letter and its door gave a bang as I let go.

That night I got a fever; my body shuddered and ached as I lay in my bed. I looked at my white cross-stitched moose and at the map, and the sea looked so alive, even though it was drawn. I sensed that Urban and Ulf were in the room, and I felt their hands on my forehead. Birgitta came in with medicine and the throbbing walls stopped throbbing and I slipped into sleep and I saw the pastor's sons standing in a line and they were singing and it was the end of humanity they were singing about. It was Daniel,

Josef, and Benjamin, those were their names; they were standing before the river in pyjamas, singing like this, along with the river, before they suddenly dove in and disappeared. Did I believe in the suffering God, they asked me under the water, could my body lend itself to the one who was highest up, and who watched over us all? What did I really know about mercy, they sang. Did I ever sing praise to the living God, they sang, along with the roaring river.

The letter. The letter. I woke up. Sat up in bed. It was night. The clock radio on the nightstand shone 4.43. I had sent a letter. This certainty that my father would read what I'd written. That he would first hold the envelope in his hand and then carefully open it and then read it. Read what I had written. What would the words do to him? What would he do once he had read it? Would he put the letter on the nightstand and think through the words? Would the memory of me be there, in that instant? Would he write back, or put aside the letter and never remember it? Would he remember me, his daughter? Would I disappear or be sent for? Earlier, before the letter, I could always hope, but now I had demanded a decision. I repeated that word, decision, and got out of bed.

The house was quiet, save for Sven's snores behind his door. I went up the stairs and sat at the kitchen table. Ate a rusk that had been left in the basket on the table. The brown-and-white woven runner lay neatly under it. I sucked on the rusk until it became wet and crumbly.

Then I took three sugar cubes from a little birch basket and bit them until my mouth was full of rusk crumbs and sugar. I washed it down with milk; I drank it from the carton, which I then set on the counter by the sink.

I heard the front door open, and Ulf came in. He took off his outerwear quickly, nodded at me, and went down the stairs. I heard him open Sven's door and I thought he was probably putting the car key back. I heard him go into his room. Then it was quiet in the house again.

I put on my snowmobile suit, even though it was too unwieldy, and pulled my hat onto my head and put on my mittens. Then I took my skis and clamped them on. It was cold outside; the stars were out, and the snow sparkled in the night. The snow was dry, and my skis ran well, even though there were no tracks cut. I went over a snow bank, down to the big road and across it, and then there was the forest and the trees were perfectly black, although the trail was lit even at night. I fit my skis in the tracks and let the poles do the work for the first few strokes. Then the speed took over and my legs and arms helped. My whole body was set for speed and in the first downhill slope it was as if it was laughing.

*

School was a concern. Until now I hadn't had to go with Ulf and Urban to take the school bus into the city. I had the days to myself and I had started doing embroidery along with Birgitta, and I'd gone skiing, taking long trips out along the river. But after Christmas that was all over. The school administrator, who knew Sven, of course, wanted me to go there, and Sven was thinking about which class I should start in. I could read and write, and there would be no problem with sports; it was more the social aspects, I heard him say on the phone one day.

It was decided that I would start in the sixth grade. I was a big girl, after all, and I counted my few remaining days of freedom and I was afraid. I didn't want to. I wasn't curious about the others, even though I had looked at the class in Ulf's and Urban's school catalogue several times. The pastor's youngest, Benjamin, was in it, and so was Anna-Lisa's daughter Britta, who always came to the IOGT meetings. Well, many of the others did too, but maybe not every time like Anna-Lisa and Britta. Anna-Lisa was a friend of Birgitta's, although she looked with such devotion at Sven as he stood there at the lectern. Britta was a girl I should become friends with, said Birgitta.

'A nice girl, a gymnast, very plucky,' said Birgitta, who secretly hoped that Britta and Ulf would get together.

After all, she didn't know anything about

the girl Ulf visited at night. Britta had her own sort of beauty, an unusual sort. I liked to look at her from different angles as we sat together in the meeting hall. From one direction, her mouth looked large and her nose was thick. From another angle, she looked sweetly doll-like; from a third, completely ordinary, just a bit pale. It was exciting to see such a changeable face, and it wasn't until I had studied her face that I discovered my own in the mirror one day.

I had two sides, I thought. The left side was dainty, almost small, like my mouth. My right side was coarser, and yet my face was held together by my green eyes and my eyebrows, which were bushy and dark. Birgitta had said that I was a beautiful girl. But that wasn't what I was looking for. I tried to remember my father's face in the instant we had looked at each other in complete calm. I remembered his sad green eyes, but everything else was hard to call forth. I remembered his chin. That it stood out a little. And his mouth. That it looked like mine.

I thought about school. Saw myself walking into the classroom and sitting down at a desk. I thought that I would probably be introduced by the teacher, but then I would be left on my own. I knew that they were afraid of me. That they talked about me at home. I understood that I would be lonesome. Of course, I was lonesome now too. But this lonesomeness would be different. It was one thing to be alone all day with only Birgitta to talk to, and another thing to be alone among many. This is a war, I thought. You are going to war. I don't know where the word *war* came from, but once it was there it couldn't be replaced by any other word. War. This is a war. I must become stronger. So strong that I won't be the one who is alone, rather those who avoid me will. The loneliness in me must become the loneliness in them. I decided to put as much effort as I could into my schoolwork. I would learn everything. It wouldn't be hard. Not if I wanted it. I decided to want to start school. By wanting it myself, I would transform the rules. I would win. This calmed me. The anxiety I had felt disappeared and was replaced by a peace I had only, until now, experienced after skiing. I just needed my father, I thought, and I realized that this was true. That Birgitta's questioning looks came out of this: that I didn't need them.

'I'm so glad you are here, Anna,' Birgitta said as I came up to breakfast.

She placed plates and spoons on the table, and I set the places. I fetched cups for tea, and small spoons. Birgitta put out the breadbasket with the freshly-baked breakfast pastries and butter and marmalade. She liked English breakfasts. Once she and Sven had gone to London, just the two of them. They had been young. That was before the children. They had stayed at a hotel and eaten English breakfasts in the morning and drunk afternoon tea in the afternoons. They had seen a musical too: *Jesus Christ Superstar*, and they had bought the recording.

'It was totally fantastic, you see,' she had said one day, and she stood close to me and showed me the album. 'Do you want me to play it?'

The music streamed out of the speakers, and when Jesus sang from the cross I tried to follow along with the text that was written down in the liner notes, but I couldn't speak English so the words didn't mean anything. But the music was beautiful. Completely different from the psalms of the Pentecostal church.

'It's so nice to have a girl in the house. It's so nice to have you. I was thinking about that when I met with Erik, and he said we should all be glad that you've come. That you're a blessing. That's what he said.'

Erik is the pastor in the Pentecostal church, and he's the one who takes care of matters of the spirit in the village. Sven is more in charge of the body and the mind. That's how they had divided it up between them, so that neither got in the way of the other. There was nothing more important than neighbourliness up here, and the community centre and the church were right next to each other. Erik and Sven sometimes planned the schedule together so that nothing conflicted with anything else, or so that the congregation could move on to the temperance meeting right after church, or vice versa.

'And he's right about that, Erik is,' she continued. 'He's so good with words. I hadn't thought of that. That you were a blessing. I had more been thinking that it makes me happy to look at you. Things like that. But blessing. That's a much better word.'

I didn't know what to say to that, so I just kept setting the table. I got the napkins and put them out; I took the boiling saucepan and poured the water into the teapot. *Blessing*, I thought, watching the way the water in the pot turned reddish-brown. *Is that what I am?* Well, Erik ought to know.

The letter came on the fourth day.

I sneaked the letter under my shirt, secured it in my waistband, and tried to walk normally past Birgitta, who was sitting on the sofa with her cross-stitching. My heart was pounding hard; it was as if it had fallen down into my stomach and was beating there, and my field of vision was white. My mouth was dry; I could hardly breathe. It was a kind of fear. As if everything had been erased, except for my heartbeat. I took the few steps from the stairs into my room and it was like walking many miles.

I closed the door and sat down on the bed. I lifted my shirt and took out the letter. I smelled it. It smelled like warm paper and cigarettes. I was far too frightened to open the letter. I needed to read it in peace, I thought, begging my heart to stop striking me.

I lay on my stomach in the bed, breathing slowly in and out. The pillow smelled like laundry detergent and hair. I squeezed my eyes closed as hard as I could. I tensed my whole body, my fists, my face, and I lay like that for several seconds before I relaxed and felt my body slowly returning to itself.

I turned onto my back in the bed. I fixed my eyes on the map. I read the words of cities and islands: Thessaloniki, Thasos, Cephalonia, Ithaca, and, far out in the sea, Cyprus.

I sat up and took the letter. Opened it with my index finger and wriggled out the piece of paper, which was covered in inked letters.

I started reading:

Something happened when we came out of the movie theatre yesterday, me and Rolf. I lit a cigarette and after that a person came and ran into the cigarette so the cigarette fell out of my hand. But the question was, where did it fall? And we looked and checked and didn't find the cigarette and then Rolf said that did it fall in your pocket then? And sure enough we found out it was in the right pocket of my jacket and had burned a hole there and we got so worked up, both of us, that we didn't talk all night. I even hung up all my clothes in the bathroom at the hospital, I thought that if anything else is burning in them they should be hanging in the bathroom.

I read the letter several times. I examined every word to try to find something in the words, or behind them. Some message to me, but I didn't find anything. My heart was still beating like a fist inside my stomach. What did it really say? He had been to the movies with Rolf. Was that the Rolf that Ulf had talked about? Was he allowed to leave the hospital? If he was, that would be good news. And he went to the movies. He went to the movies and he smoked cigarettes. He was afraid of fire.

I thought that he was describing an incident that must have happened recently. I got the paper and paged to the movie listings at the very back. At the Grand, there was a spy film showing in the big theatre and a Western in the small one. Which film had he seen? I guessed the Western.

I made two decisions: I would write another letter and I would go to the movies on Saturday. I absolutely wanted to go by myself. I could take the bus into the city, but if I wasn't allowed, I would have to take Ulf or Urban. Preferably Urban.

I put the letter aside, in the nightstand drawer, and sneaked upstairs with the paper.

I had never been to the movies. It made

me happy that I would soon be watching the same film my father had seen the week before. I thought about how I would present my visit to the movie theatre to Sven and Birgitta. Surely they would want someone to go with me. But it was also possible that they would encourage me to go on my own. I had been listening to them one evening when they were talking to each other about how it wasn't good for me to be in the house so much. That I ought to spend time on a hobby that wasn't just skiing. A team sport. Volleyball, they had decided, and Sven would talk to the coach.

I would bring it up with Birgitta while we were sewing. That always put her in a good mood. The worst that could happen was that she would say she wanted to come along. Maybe I would go on a Sunday, when she was busy with the coffee and cookies for temperance. On the other hand, I felt sure—why, I didn't know—that Conrad had been allowed to leave the hospital on a Saturday. Maybe I would meet him there. At the movie theatre.

*

Ulf came and got me. I was lying on my bed, looking at the map. By now I knew the names of all the Greek islands and the cities on the mainland.

'Come on,' he said. 'Daniel, Joseph, and Benjamin are here. We're going to the church.'

I didn't ask why, I just sat up in bed and followed him into the hall. I put on my down coat and my hat and tied on my winter boots. It was fifteen below outside, and the steam moved in and out of my mouth. I nodded at the pastor's sons, who were standing in a row on the street, waiting for us.

Still without speaking to one another, we walked up the hill to the Pentecostal church. Daniel opened it with a key. I had never been in the church when there was no one there. The wooden pews gaped, empty. The hymnals were piled on a wooden table, and at the very front was the altarpiece with the crucified Jesus. I trembled inside. As if from excitement. But I didn't know if that's what it was.

'Put her there,' said Daniel, who was the oldest, pointing at the pulpit.

Ulf held my arm, and together we walked to the pulpit. He stationed me there and turned me around, out toward the empty rows of pews. The pastor's sons stood at the very back, and Ulf went to them and he sat down too.

'Now you can begin,' said Daniel.

I looked at them. Four blond-haired boys looking at me with their eyes. What did they want? What was I supposed to begin doing? My legs shook because they were looking at me like that. I wanted to go. Sit down with them and laugh it all off, but I kept standing there.

'What should I begin doing?' I asked.

'You're going to speak in tongues,' said Daniel.

There was no one in the congregation who spoke in tongues. I had heard Erik say that he was very careful about the truth, so no one in his church was allowed to fake things.

'I can't do it either, and I'm a pastor,' he

said. That's how careful he was. 'God is the one who should speak through people', he had said. 'And we don't play with God's words. Either they're there, or they're not. We can do nothing more than pray, read the texts, and hope. But we must never misrepresent ourselves. Never make things up for His sake.'

What had he said? That I should let God speak through me?

'I can't,' I said.

'Try.'

Daniel sounded stern. Sometimes it seemed as if he was the one who was in charge in that family. Even Erik seemed weak beside him.

I decided to try. It burned inside me. Why? Shame? I stood there on the floor, ashamed. Then I opened my mouth and spoke.

The words gushed forth; there was no beginning and no end to the words; they hung together and played with each other, drawing themselves out and pushing back inside my mouth. The whole church was full of them; they roared and rushed like the river, I thought, and it was as if I were viewing them from a distance and as if I could see how they played with one another. Biting one another and pushing away. Never before had I felt the way I did now, with the church full of words that came out of me, from the deepest parts of me.

They came and painted everything around them blue. They whirled, and I dove into the waves. I saw a girl lying in a bed, asleep; her hair was spread over the pillow. I bent down to her to stroke her cheek. Then she opened her eyes. I fell through a tunnel and woke up lying on the floor. The pastor's sons and Ulf were bent over me.

'I told you she could do it,' said Ulf.

My life changed. Every Sunday I spoke in tongues, if that was indeed what I was doing when the words came, seeming to pour out of my mouth, the only thing that was real. The words that intertwined and sang. The services were always well-attended and the rumours had spread all the way up to the surrounding cities.

School was no longer in question, Erik had said. 'It's important for her to rest, as much strength as it takes. You see, she gives us great parts of herself every time she speaks. She's not like the rest of us. I can tutor her myself, in the Holy Scripture,' Erik told Sven, but Sven said no to that. She didn't have to be religious just because she spoke in tongues. Sven and Erik sized each other up.

I continued to send letters to Conrad, even if I didn't get anything in return. I described what I did all day, but I kept it to myself, the part about speaking in tongues. I wasn't sure that it was God speaking, and I wanted to wait until I knew more. Besides, I sensed that part would worry Conrad. He probably had enough going on with his own voices. I looked up schizophrenia in the dictionary. Serious psychological illness with intellectual deterioration. I thought about the voices for a long time. About how my strange voice was healthy, even valuable, while his was sick and meant that he had to be locked up in a hospital. I thought about how our different voices might be alike. That maybe the differences weren't as great as they had seemed at first.

I got to go to the movies on the third Saturday after the first letter came. I took the bus into the city. I got to go by myself, as I had hoped.

The Grand was next to the shopping centre, near the sea. I seldom thought about that. That the city was on the sea. Maybe that was because the downtown wasn't right next to it. But you only had to walk for five minutes and you would get to the sea. There was ice there now, and the ice-breaker was anchored at the big pier, waiting. The sun and all the white stung my eyes. I put my hands to my forehead to make enough shadow to look out across the ice, far, far away. I wanted to walk out on it, but I didn't dare—what if it cracked? I had never walked on ice before, and I felt that Urban should be with me.

I turned toward the shopping centre again, where the movie theatre was at the end. I was nervous, because maybe I would see him. Otherwise he wouldn't have had to give me a clue like this.

I went up to the window, where an older woman was reading a paper.

'One ticket to the Western,' I said, 'and a soda and also a bag of candy.'

There were pre-bagged candies in a basket. I was the only one there, but that wasn't too strange, because I was early. I didn't know how long it would take to get from the bus stop to the movie theatre, and also I wanted to be early so I could carefully study the people who came.

The first people to come were two boys in hats and down coats. I just observed that they were there, and then I kept my eyes on the door. It opened two more times. Two girls, older than me, and three senior citizens from the nursing home showed up. All of them were going to see the spy film, so when the doors to the theatres opened I entered the small one on my own. I took off my down coat and started eating my candy. It tasted fantastic. I sucked carefully on them one piece at a time before I started on the next. I was at a matinee. This was a new word; it was written outside the theatre.

The daily matinee showing.

I leaned back when the movie started. I wasn't disappointed that my father hadn't come. It almost felt nice to have the room to myself, and when the music and the moving images started I was happy. I almost said it aloud. I'm at the movies and I am happy.

When I came home, I wrote a long letter to my father in which I recounted my experience of the whole film. I thought that maybe he forgets, so he watches the same film over and over again. I asked him to come next Saturday, so we could see it again together, and then I asked him to send a photo from when he was little. I had heard Sven talking about how his aunt had dementia and that all she remembered were small scenes from her childhood. The time she got a dollhouse for her birthday; her father had made it and decorated it with furniture and everything—and her confirmation, she could remember that. The time the pastor gave her the wafer and Jesus's blood to drink. That she hadn't liked the taste of the blood and wanted to spit it out, but she forced herself to swallow. Maybe Conrad too only remembers his childhood. Maybe I have to start there and then coax out the memory of my birth.

I was already starting to get nervous for the next day, when I would stand before the congregation. I was afraid that nothing would come, no words, and that people would be disappointed. I wanted to do my best, since they were coming for me, and from far away too. Once I had seen Greta sitting in the congregation, but when the service was over she wasn't there. I would have liked to have asked her about Conrad. I wanted nothing more than to return to the house. My armour. Was it still in the kitchen bench? Did someone else live there now? I wanted to know. I hoped that she would come next Sunday, but I never saw her again.

Sunday came; Erik dressed me in the shift and asked me, as he usually did, not to feign anything.

'If it comes, it comes. You don't have to do

this for the sake of anyone but yourself. And if you don't want to, you don't want to. Take it as it comes. Just follow along with the service. After the confession of faith I'll nod at you, and then it's your turn. We'll do what we usually do, right?'

Erik took me by the chin and looked into my eyes. His eyes were brown, and I didn't look away. Never, for him.

'You are a blessing. A miracle. But we must never let it weigh you down. You must never be made to bear anything more than your age allows. Do you hear what I'm saying?'

'Yes,' I said.

'Are you very tired afterwards?'

I nodded.

I woke in Erik's arms. He carried me into the pastor's room, where he would go to change his clothes, and he laid me down on four chairs, which stood next to each other along the wall.

He crouched next to me, stroked my hair several times, and whispered, 'You were good today. You were really good.'

The next day I received another letter. I shouted with joy inside when I saw it lying on the floor of the hall. I took it and forgot to hide it. I just ran down the stairs and into my room. I kicked the door closed behind me and threw myself onto the bed, ripping open the envelope. A black-and-white photograph fell out and I held it in my hand and looked at it for a long time before I started reading the letter.

This is a picture of my mom when we swam in Lake Österjörn, seventy kilometres inland from Skellefteå. I don't remember this day, but I remember we swam in the same spot many times, but I don't remember this particular day. My mom is named Gerda and then there's my siblings Göran and Märta and then there's me. And my mom and my dad got divorced so she had to work in a meatpacking plant and didn't make very much money, but it was enough for three children and for her.

We had a sewing machine in the bedroom, of course, and that's where Göran came up with, my brother, that he would have a fort

with soldiers so he was just out in the sand-
box getting a lot of sand to scatter over the
sewing machine, it never worked again of
course, but he got his fort there, he always
got to keep it on the sewing machine.

He had answered my question. So the childhood thing worked. He had sent a photograph as I had asked him to. Conrad had siblings. Göran and Märta. Where were they now?

I looked at the photograph. My father is squinting at the sun and looking at the camera. Märta and Göran are playing with a boat.

He was just a child, but I could recognize him. I recognized him and I recognized myself. There was something similar about our eyes and cheekbones. It was obvious. It wasn't my imagination, or a longing. The similarity was there. I rushed into Urban's room with the photograph. He was lying there reading the Bible, as usual.

'Urban,' I called, 'look at this, Urban.'

I threw myself down on his bed and held out the photograph.

Urban slowly put his Bible down on the nightstand. He sat up and gave me a look that I didn't bother to interpret. He looked at the photograph for a long time.

'Is that Conrad?' he asked, pointing at my father.

'Yes. Yes,' I said. 'There's Conrad and Märta and Göran and then that's their mom, Gerda.'

'Urban,' I said. 'Don't we look alike?'

Urban looked carefully and for a long time at Conrad as a child. Then he said, 'Sure you do. Can you leave now?'

I went back to my own room. Delighted at this confirmed similarity. I looked like him. He looked like me.

I felt a rush from all of this likeness. I wanted to scream out loud. Just roar, without anyone hearing me. I had to get out. Out of the house, to my skis. I changed and ran up the stairs. Birgitta's 'dinner in fifteen minutes' slid right off me. Out. Out. I didn't bother with my jacket, I just grabbed my hat and mittens. I ran to the garage door where my skis were leaning and clamped them on. I went up the hill fast and soon I was in the tracks and there, finally, the scream could come. I skied and cried and screamed. I screamed louder than I ever had before, and it was as if my body had just been waiting to get to scream, all these weeks with the family in the village. It was a scream as mighty as a skyscraper, a wall of water, like the river in the spring, like an aircraft that tears loose and takes off. I screamed until every cell inside me vibrated. My scream was like a storm. Like pouring rain. My scream was like a spear. Like a way out.

I shovelled down the meat and potatoes when I came home. There was still a plate for me on the table, and Birgitta looked at me curiously. Both Sven and Birgitta had started doing that ever since this voice thing in church. Sometimes I thought that it was like they were afraid of me. Familiarity had been exchanged for distance. The small talk at the dinner table seemed to have vanished unnoticed, and I think I missed it. I really wanted to be like a daughter in this house, even if everyone knew I wasn't. After dinner I closed myself in my room again. I looked at the photograph again and again, as if it could tell me something more than what I already knew. My father's dark hair, his way of tilting his head to the side.

I went into the bathroom with the photograph and held it up beside my face. I arranged my face so it tilted exactly like his. Then I squinted and pulled up my mouth so my teeth were visible. The similarity was striking. How old was Conrad in the picture? Eight years old. He could have been my little brother.

I wrote another letter that evening. I had bought a piece of stationery with the envelope. The stationery was white with the royal seal of three crowns. I had chosen between one with horses on it and the one with the three crowns, but I decided the crowns suited Conrad better. I wrote only one sentence. A question:

What do you do all day?
    Your daughter

I thought it was good to keep it simple, so he didn't have too much to react to.

I sealed the envelope. Once again I went to the kiosk with the letter inside my jacket. I bought the stamp from the woman in the kiosk and this time I had a few extra *kronor* for candy. I bought three diamond candies, one for me and one for Urban and one for Ulf. They were beautiful, red and green and big. They would last all night. I mailed the letter and walked home. I met Anna-Lisa and Britta on the way. They were out walking with their dog; it was a Siberian husky. I had seen it many times and I thought it was beautiful with its ice-blue eyes and black eyelashes. I wanted to have a dog, a dog just like that was what I wanted, but I had never dared to ask Birgitta or Sven. Anna-Lisa nodded and I walked over to them. Britta looked at me from under her hat and I said hi.

'Anna,' said Anna-Lisa. 'Wouldn't you like to come to our house sometime? Britta would like that, wouldn't you, Britta.'

Britta looked at me and nodded.

'You can spend time in Britta's room and

take the dog out,' said Anna-Lisa.

'Sure,' I said. 'We could do that.'

I only said it to get away, but as resolute as Anna-Lisa was I would surely have to visit.

'Goodbye,' I said, and I turned onto the street and then up the hill to the house.

Damn, I thought when I thought about Britta. I wanted to think about my father instead. About how he would receive the letter the next day. I wanted to think about Conrad and the diamonds I was bringing home; instead I was thinking about what it might look like in Britta's room. About what we would say to each other. *People take up so much space in a person*, I thought. *They eat their way in and stay, even though you want to be alone. What does Britta's look from under her hat do in my body?* I knew that only the skis could make her disappear now that she was there, but I couldn't go skiing tonight. Tonight we were going to have tea, all of us together. Urban wasn't going to practice and Ulf wasn't with the pastor's sons. We would drink tea and have a family meeting. I had never been to one of them, but I had heard of them. Everyone would contribute to the family meeting with their thoughts and experiences. We would discuss the family's important issues.

When I came in, everyone was already sitting around the kitchen table. I hurried to take off my jacket and shoes. I slid down onto a chair with the bag of candy in my hand.

'It's good that you're here,' said Sven. 'I have a list of speakers here, with the topics we're going to discuss. If there's anything in particular you want us to talk about, write it down here.' He handed me the list, which was full of questions. I tried to think of something I could bring up, but I couldn't come up with anything, so I handed the list back to Sven.

'Item one: this is from Birgitta and me, and the heading is "silence." We feel that we don't talk to each other anymore. As if everyone is so deeply involved in their own thing that there's not much of a sense of togetherness left in our family. No team spirit. We were talking about this the other day, Birgitta and me, and we realized that we miss you. What do you think, Urban?'

Urban took a sip of his tea and raked his fingers through his hair.

'That time has passed, Dad,' Urban said, and he buttered a rusk.

'What do you mean by that, Urban?' Sven asked in a friendly voice.

'It's been a long time since you were that close to us,' Urban continued. 'It's been a long time since we turned to you when we had a question about something. It's completely natural,' he added.

'Does anyone else have something to say? Birgitta?'

'Well, I think it's sad when no one says anything,' said Birgitta. 'Only Ulf does, and with you, Ulf, it feels like you think you have to because no one else does.'

'Have to what?' said Ulf.

'Well, you're always joking with me,' said Birgitta. 'About how I just sit on the couch embroidering. You know, things like that. You don't have to do that for my sake. I'll be okay. I'd rather that we talk to each other because we actually want to.'

I had never heard Birgitta speak for so long and so coherently.

I looked out the window, because suddenly I had tears in my eyes, and they were for Birgitta. Because what she longed for would never happen. Then there was something about how they became so small, Sven and Birgitta, that I didn't like. It was unpleasant to feel bigger than them. Like Urban, Ulf and I were bigger, when it ought to be the other way around.

'Don't worry about me, Mom,' Ulf said, and when he said it Birgitta started to cry.

'Let's move on,' said Urban, looking at the list of items. 'Make dinner together,' he read aloud.

'Yes,' said Sven. 'That's Birgitta's idea, and I must say that I think it's an excellent one. We'll cook dinner together once a week. And we'll take turns being responsible for the meal. One person will do the shopping and decide what to eat, and then we'll all help make it. What do you say?'

'Okay,' said Urban, as if he knew that he had to go along with his parents for their sake.

'Okay,' said Ulf, looking at me.

'Okay,' I said, nodding appreciatively.

'Oh, how nice,' said Birgitta. 'Then we'll pick a day—Wednesdays. I'll start. I can think of something unusual, something exotic. Then we'll meet here in the kitchen at five o'clock and begin.'

No one said anything.

'The next item is a quick one,' said Sven. 'Personal hygiene. You ought to shower more often. In fact, this goes for all three of you, and that's why I'm bringing it up so openly. Shower and wash up every day, and it's a requirement after practice. So that's that. The next item is how messy the dirty laundry is. Shape up. And now Ulf has an item.'

Urban and I stared at Ulf.

'The car,' he said. 'I think we should get a new car. The one we have is too small, now that Anna's here. The engine is bad too,' he said, putting a sugar cube between his teeth. Then he filtered his tea through the sugar cube as he looked at us one by one.

'I see. The next item is perhaps a bit more serious,' said Sven, looking at me. 'Anna, we feel that you should do things with other people. That it's no longer enough for you to stay here at home. You know that I'm not too happy about all this Pentecostal church stuff, and I've spoken to Erik and he thinks it's a good idea too. A team sport, Anna. You know what I'm talking about. You're starting volleyball on Monday.'

Was that all, I thought, not understanding why Sven was being so serious. I had thought it was school, so I was definitely a little relieved.

'Does that sound good?' he asked.

'Yes, that sounds good,' I said.

'Then we're finished,' said Sven, at which Urban and Ulf stood up and went down the stairs and into their rooms.

I wanted to go too, but there was that part about Birgitta being lonely, so I remained seated.

'I ran into Anna-Lisa and Britta,' I tried. Birgitta lit up. 'They wanted me to come over and visit.'

'Why, you want to, right?' said Birgitta. 'How nice. When are you supposed to go?'

'We're supposed to talk later,' I said, and it

felt like I was giving her a present, something really nice that she'd wanted for a long time.

'You could have a friend, Anna,' she said, placing her hand on mine and searching for my eyes. 'That means a lot. More than you might think.'

After this at least I could go, I thought, and I stood up.

'Thanks, Anna,' Birgitta said, and she stood up too.

I walked down the stairs with the bag of candy in my hand. I knocked on Urban's door and went in. Urban was sitting on his bed with his legs pulled up, leaning against the wall.

'I have candy. Do you want some?' I said, holding out the bag with the diamonds.

'Damn it, Anna.'

I looked at him, sitting there on the bed. What did he say?

'What do you mean?'

'Volleyball and Britta. It's wrong, do you understand?'

'What's right, then?' I asked, not daring to look at him anymore.

'You don't speak in tongues,' he said, looking at me for so long that I eventually met his gaze. 'You know that, right?'

*

We were sitting on Britta's bed. Her bedspread was a patchwork quilt in various shades of pink, and she had pink curtains. A small chandelier hung from the ceiling, and the glass reflected against the walls, seeming to dance. Everything was very orderly and beautiful. As orderly as Britta's hair, which was always done up in elaborate styles. Today she had a ballerina bun. To go with that, she had a pink Bambi shirt and a burgundy corduroy skirt. She had pink slippers on her feet.

I felt awkward in my brown shirt and my jeans, and I thought I felt that way because I was sitting here with Britta. I had never felt this way at other times.

'If you went to school we could be in the same class,' Britta said.

'I don't go to school,' I said.

'Why not?' Britta asked.

'I don't really know. I have enough to do with church, I think.'

Inside, I felt that everything I took for granted would seem strange here in Britta's room. It was as if the person I was and the life I lived couldn't tolerate questions. I felt weakened. Yes, that particular word came to me. I saw myself running in a meadow, chased by archers. The arrows slammed down around me, and I knew that a single arrow would be enough to bring me to the ground. One arrow, and I would lie there dying in the grass. I would bleed to death, and nothing of what I knew would be near me. Suddenly I felt fragile. Through Britta's eyes, I looked like a lost girl. My father had slipped away and turned into a shadow, far away. I had nothing, here on Britta's bed. I was all on my own, and it seemed like Britta was several hundred people.

'Do you touch yourself when you're in bed alone?' she asked.

'What do you mean?' I asked, looking out the window. It was dark out, as usual, and I thought about the spring that would come. About what Urban had said about the river's happiness and the light that comes so quickly that people go crazy. Sun-sick, Urban called it, when you couldn't sleep because you just kept climbing higher and higher. The happiness that would settle in you and didn't have room in your body so it went out through your head and made a hole. 'That's why you should wear a hat until June,' he had said. 'To keep your head together.'

'You know, when you're naked under the covers. Between your legs?'

'No,' I said.

'Haven't you ever done it?' she asked eagerly.

I wanted to go home. Home.

'Haven't you?' she asked again.

'No,' I said, although I didn't know what she was talking about.

There was a knock at the door. It was Anna-Lisa.

'Would you like a snack?' she asked. 'It's ready.'

It was nice to leave Britta's room. We went up the stairs and sat down at the table. Anna-Lisa had put out drinks and cookies.

She looked at me and smiled with her mouth, though her eyes were asking something I didn't understand. I tried to smile back as I took a cookie. Anna-Lisa was a widow; I knew that, and it was something special. I knew that something had happened, because Birgitta and Sven had said something about it. Something I couldn't remember now. Could I ask about it?

'Help yourself,' Anna-Lisa said.

She watched Britta and me and suddenly she looked happy. Her face, which usually guarded itself, softened. *She's so young*, I thought. *She's happy because Britta and I are together*, I thought. But of course that's not how it was. Suddenly I felt guilty because I was sitting here lying to Anna-Lisa, because I was here against my will. Because I was pretending.

'I'm going home now,' I said, standing up.

I didn't dare to look at Britta and Anna-Lisa. I went to the hall and put on my shoes and jacket. Suddenly she was there, Britta, and I gave a start when I saw her smile.

'Are you afraid of me?' she asked.

I didn't answer. I just looked at her pretty face.

'Are you?'

I shook my head. Suddenly she embraced me. Then she stood for a long time with her arms around me. I think she was crying because my jacket got wet, and finally I had to hug her back.

Anna-Lisa popped up, and her face was blotchy. She smiled at me. Stroked my hair, even though I didn't want her to.

'Come back soon,' she said. 'We'd like that. Wouldn't we, Britta?'

Britta loosened her grip on me, wiped her nose on the arm of her shirt, and looked at me with a calm I had never seen in her before.

'Yes. You should come back,' she said.

I ran all the way home. It hurt to pull the cold air into my lungs. I ran from Britta and Anna-Lisa. From Britta's face and Anna-Lisa's unhappiness. The house grew closer. I saw Ulf shovelling snow out front. He raised a hand in greeting and that gesture spread through me like warmth; it was a silent rejoicing that someone recognized me. That I belonged with them. With Sven and Birgitta and Urban and Ulf. I waved back, raising my hand at Ulf, who was smiling.

I couldn't fall asleep that night. I twisted and turned in bed with the wind outside chasing me through the hours. I really wanted to sleep. To get away from everything and then wake to a new day. I wanted to wake up, shower, and then sit down at the set table and eat Start muesli with milk, and rye with cheese, and drink tea. I wanted to talk to Sven about the Umeå team and to Birgitta about cooking. I wanted to show my gratefulness and try to please them. I'd been given so much; I wanted to give something back. Instead I thought about Sunday. We were going to have a special guest from Uppsala, and it was extra important for the voice to come as it should. Erik had said I just needed to do what I usually did, that nothing was different, but I know he didn't mean it. Never before had they had visitors from the Pentecostal church in Uppsala, and they were coming for my sake.

I received an answer the very next day. Strangely enough, seeing the letter in the mailbox didn't excite me as much as the other times. I brought in the letter and didn't even hide it; instead I carried it in my hand, as if it were a matter of course that I should receive mail. I was home alone, and maybe that could explain why I felt so calm. I had plenty of time. Birgitta was at the grocery store in town, and Urban and Ulf were at school. Sven didn't come home before six on weekdays, and besides, he was working on making a new sign for the bathhouse.

I turned into the kitchen and threw the letter on the counter with a gesture that showed me that I had no fear of what might be in it. I exchanged letters with my father, and now the next letter had arrived. It was that simple, I told myself. I put on the coffeemaker because I felt that the situation demanded something strong, and I took buns out of the bread basket. Birgitta had baked new ones with almond paste to make me happy. She was so happy about me and Britta. She had run into Anna-Lisa, who said that we got along so well. That we had sat talking to each other in Britta's room for a long time.

Why had she said that, I wondered. Was she ashamed that I had just left?

I took out a cup and poured the coffee in; I mixed in a lot of milk and sat down at the table. I let the letter lie on the counter while I drank the coffee and ate the bun. It was snowing outside. Tomorrow would be the first of December. Birgitta had already taken out the advent candles and lit the first candle, and Sven had explained that Christmas meant togetherness for the family, and that they lit candles to brighten the darkness. He didn't say anything about the birth of Jesus, but at the advent concert at church I had heard the songs about the star that shone over Bethlehem.

*

I drank the coffee, put the cup in the dish-washer, and took the letter with me down to my room.

No hammering heart. No shortness of breath. Just me and the letter from my father. I opened the envelope, took out the letter, and read:

I mostly spend my days at Balder. The day centre. We hang out with one another and play cards. Bismarck. I can pass with any high cards at all. The others don't have a chance. But I still like playing. At eleven our daytime medication comes and then it's lunch. There's nothing wrong with the food, Anna. And then, as a rule, I'm home in the ward by three, and then I help in the kitchen if I'm allowed, preparing dinner. Then it's dinner at five and then I go to bed pretty early. I don't like TV very much. Then I get up early. And then I'm on my way by about half past nine.

My name. He addressed me by name. My hands ached, as they always did before I cried. The tears tore at me, pressing out my eyes and down my cheeks. 'There's nothing wrong with the food, Anna.' Anna. Anna. I read the sentence again and again, as the tears flowed. The tears pulled me down on the bed. I cried into my pillow, sobbing now. My whole body shook with tears. 'Dad,' I said aloud in the room. 'Dad. Dad.' From now on, Sven would just be Sven. The word 'Dad' belonged to my father and me. Was it closer? I asked myself through the tears. Dad. It was like standing next to him, close, close. Dad was like a calmness, like a familiar light, like warmth, like an intimate glance.

I kept reading. It was a long letter:

My mom died when I was thirteen, and after that my life changed drastically. Göran and Märta were placed with families in Skellefteå, while I was placed with my youngest aunt, Annie, in Mölndal, and the whole family sort of dissolved.

My dad stayed in the apartment at Nygatan 95A in Skellefteå. All by himself, then. He was an alcoholic and he abused alcohol so we couldn't live with him.

I got to know a girl in Mölndal who was
in the eighth grade. And in Mölndal boys
were in one class and girls were in another.
They couldn't be in the same class. And
then I was with this girl Kerstin Berntsson,
Gustavsberg 524, Mölndal 2, for six months.
And then Annie went to figure-skating train-
ing in Vålådalen, that is my aunt who I lived
with. And then this girl and I were alone in
the apartment and then she wanted to have
sex with me. And my uncle had said that it
was really dangerous, you could have a kid,
so I said no, I said. And then she threatens
me somehow and then I said then I'll go
home to Skellefteå, I told her. And then she
said this: you wouldn't dare. And just
because she said it I packed my bags and I
went to Skellefteå and I remember at a rail-
way junction I dropped off a letter to the
school that I had quit. And so I came back
to Skellefteå when I was fourteen.
All of us siblings moved into the apartment
at Nygatan 95. Our dad, Birger, had moved
to the outskirts of the city. And we didn't
have an adult, but we got help from Jansson
the social-services clerk, who was from

Bureå. That was twenty kilometres north of Skellefteå. She made food for us, and from Jansson we got three coats, one for each of us.

I worked at the brewery in the summers, and I got drinks, three a day so that was twenty-one a week, and they liked that, Göran and Märta. We weren't very spoiled. And then I started going to dances when I was about seventeen, and of course there was quite a bit of alcohol along with those dance evenings. So I remember one night I didn't want to go home to Göran and Märta, so I climbed up into the attic. There was a little opening at the very top, where there was a chain-link fence, and I slept there. Then I came down once I'd sobered up.

Alcohol, I thought. *Sex?* I read the letter again before I put it back in the envelope.

Birgitta came in the front door. I heard the rustle of bags and her 'hello.'

I called 'hello' back, opened the drawer of the nightstand, and placed the letter inside with the others.

I have to meet him, I thought.

'We're going to make Indonesian chicken curry,' Birgitta said seriously, looking at us one by one.

All five of us were gathered in the kitchen. Urban and Ulf, Sven, Birgitta, and me.

'I've bought the ingredients and started cooking the chicken, but we'll do the rest together,' said Birgitta.

Everything was lined up on the counter. Cream, bouillon, leeks, spices, peanuts.

'Ulf and Sven can make the sauce. I stuck the recipe up on the cupboard door. Urban, you can start by setting the table, and then you can debone the chicken. Anna, you're in charge of the condiments. Look at the recipe. I'll make the fruit salad and help everyone out.'

Everyone made an effort for Birgitta's sake. It felt to me like it was important to keep going all the time; stopping to think might ruin everything. The next movement and the next, so Birgitta wouldn't go to pieces. She had invested so much. *It has to work*, I thought, and I watched Ulf work on with the sauce, mixing bouillon and cream with the curry. It was as if everyone instinctively understood the gravity of the situation. Urban carved the meat of the chicken with his own filet knife, the one he usually used on the fish; Sven chopped the leeks. I sneaked a look at Birgitta's taut jaw and shiny eyes while I sliced bananas and placed them in a bowl. Then the coconut flakes and the peanuts and the mango chutney.

Birgitta lit the candles and decorated the table with flowers. For dessert we were going to have exotic fruit. Papaya, mango, pineapple.

'What's this?' Sven said, holding up something that looked like an orange cherry.

'Ground cherries,' said Birgitta. 'They're from Sri Lanka.'

When everything was on the table, Birgitta started to cry. Ulf groaned loudly and Urban seemed to collapse into himself.

'It's really good, Birgitta,' I said. 'It's the best thing I've ever eaten.'

It was true. It tasted wonderful. And I wanted her to stop crying.

'I'm just happy,' she cried. 'You're all so lovely. I'm sorry.'

'Our faith in God gives us hope. Hope that all people can experience atonement and communion with God. Hope that no situation in life is so difficult that God cannot change it. Hope for redress for our inner selves as well as our bodies and the relationships we live in. A redress that we can taste even now, but which has its fulfilment on the other side of the grave when we will meet God face-to-face. This hope means healing for our entire world, in the belief that Jesus will come back.'

I was sitting in the room off the nave, listening to Erik's introduction. My insides were twisting and turning. My hands were shaking. Birgitta had brushed my hair and arranged it in two braids, and dressed me in a grey flannel skirt, a white blouse, and a thin, knitted red sweater. Erik had placed me in the innermost room long before he went to greet the congregation. He didn't want me to notice how full the church was. I wasn't meant to see him welcoming the Pentecostal pastor from Uppsala. Everything is just like always, he had repeated time and again, as if to convince himself that it was so. But it wasn't. Everything was different. I was to be on display. Erik would impress the Pentecostal pastor who had travelled all the way up here to listen to me. Erik had asked Sven if he could take me to Uppsala, but Sven had said no to that.

Now they were singing about the angels in heaven and about hell, where you would burn if you didn't have the correct faith in Jesus Christ.

Then Erik would pray for the congregation. Then it was me.

The edges of my vision were burning as I approached the lectern. My tongue felt rough and sluggish, as if it were too large for my mouth. The red moved behind my eyelids each time I blinked. It was as if I didn't dare to blink because the red was there, but in the end I had to, of course. Erik led me by the arm; it was like he was holding me up, like I couldn't walk without him. I didn't dare to look at the congregation, even if I could sense its presence. I knew that the church was full, so full that many people were standing. I looked down at the floor, and it was as if he were dragging me, Erik. My legs were soft and didn't follow me. I had to tell my body what to do: blink, one more step, and then another. Up at the lectern I hugged myself so hard that my knuckles turned white. I nodded at Selma at the organ.

The words came. I sobbed with relief. They came powerfully, and it was as if I were always a step behind the words, as if they pulled me after them. I didn't have time to swallow, because the words were in the way and they wanted out. They pounded out of me like tears, and they came so intensely that I had to cry out. I cried out in the church and I thought about the pastor from Uppsala and Sven and Birgitta and the boys who were sitting there somewhere and I didn't want anything to do with the dizziness that came because I was with the words that didn't cease. We held each other's hands and walked across a large meadow. It was windy and the light was so bright that we squinted at the sun and there, far off, were bronzed mountains and we walked in those mountains all the way to where the sea was waiting. We fell. Fell together, down into the sea.

When I woke up I was once again lying in the small room within the nave. Erik bent over me and I looked into his eyes and thought: *never. Never again.*

Sven came, and Birgitta and Ulf and Urban. They all crowded into the small room and from far away I heard Sven talking to Erik about how this couldn't be good for me. He was agitated. And yet his voice didn't penetrate to me as I lay there looking up at the whitewashed ceiling. There was some strong smell in there, and I tried to figure out what it was. Ulf crouched down beside me where I lay on the wooden pew. He smiled, I could feel that. It was a smile that hit me in the face, where it flowed out and warmed me.

'Anna,' he whispered. 'Anna. I love you.'

What did he say? Suddenly he was gone and Urban crouched down and sought my gaze.

'Anna. How are you?' He spoke slowly, as always. 'Anna, I have to talk to you about what the pastor said. The church is empty.

Everyone has gone home, Anna. I'm going to tell you, but first you have to get up.'

Urban's voice. I think that was what I liked the very most. His manner of shaping his lips around the words; it seemed both careful and beautiful. There was no doubt inside him; everything was ready in there. He took my hands and pulled me up so I was sitting in the pew. He crouched before me, didn't let go of my hands.

'Anna. I wasn't supposed to hear them talking to each other. The pastor and the other one from Uppsala. I was standing right next to them.'

His eyes, tearing into me. Urban and me, alone, with the others on the fringes.

I was listening to him now. To the words and the tone of them. The whole room was singing. We looked at each other, and our eyes held each other. It was an instant that lasted for eternity. When the words came, it was as if they were falling from the sky.

'It's not tongues you're speaking, Anna. It's Greek.'

PART TWO

I REMEMBER THE taxi ride. And the room we came into. Urban's hand on my shoulder. How he squeezed it. Calmly. As calmly as only he could do, and we sat down on two vinyl chairs. Three people came into the room. They introduced themselves to me and I stared at them, trying to understand what they were saying. I hadn't seen anyone outside the family for a long time, and they were so bright. So bright, with their coats and their hair combed back neatly.

'My name is Bengt,' said one. 'I'm a senior physician here. Your brother is very worried about you.'

'Mats, I'm an intern.'

He was blond and smiled with the teeth he had. I was afraid of him. His upper body swayed this way and that as he sat down in his chair. The room had woven curtains that fought to cover the windows, but still a beam of light came in and cut across the senior physician, seeming to cut him in two, and I thought that he had a bright and a dark side.

The last person to introduce himself was Artan. He was a nurse here, he said in a voice that vibrated in the room. It was a voice you wanted to listen to, I had time to think as they sat before us like three judges and I was the one who would be judged. How had I ended up here?

Urban had gotten me dressed and said that we were going to the hospital, that there was nothing else we could do. He begged me to trust him. He had spoken to them on the phone.

'Like I said, your brother is very worried.

Can you tell us how you feel?'

This question was directed at me; it flew through the room like a spear.

'Can you tell us?' Bengt asked, crossing one leg over the other. He stared at me, forcing me to close my eyes. Bengt, Mats, and Artan wandered behind my eyelids like phantoms. They floated in the room and it was Urban's hand that brought me back. He embraced me suddenly and tightly. He held onto me as if he would never let go, and that's probably what he was saying with the embrace. I won't let you go. I will never let you go. I opened my eyes again. They were sitting still in their chairs, and it was as if they had doubled, as if there were at least six of them there before me.

'My sister hasn't spoken for a long time,' I heard my brother saying, far off.

'How long has it been since you've spoken?'

I tried to loosen something in my throat, something that was in the way. I thought that he would hit me, Bengt, if I couldn't. I looked at Artan, who met my gaze without wanting anything from me. But then, when I closed my eyes again, Urban squeezed my hand hard.

'We're all here to help you,' said Bengt, and the intern and Artan nodded in agreement.

Urban looked at me. How he looked at me, with tears hanging there in his eyes.

I looked at the door behind them. The door I'd come in through. How had that happened? I had no memory of coming in through that door. Had they carried me? I looked at Urban. He was looking at me seriously. As if he were trying to tell me something with his eyes, something the others couldn't hear. I should stay here, he said. That was what he was saying. No more than that. I heard the words pushing out through his eyes; I saw them like colours. He coloured the room red with his plea. He was imploring me. I looked and looked at him. It was all I could do. There was nothing more than him. That's how it was, and it could never be any other way.

'So you can't speak,' said Bengt.

He turned to the intern: 'Speech latency

non-existent.' Bengt wrote on a notepad. His pen scratched inside me, cutting me up inside, and I could see the blood streaming out of me.

'Can you help me die?'

I uttered this wish into the room, loudly and distinctly. It came from the very deepest part of me, and it bounced around from wall to wall. I knew that it was what I wanted, and now that I knew it I would never forget.

Bengt leaned forward. He tried to catch my gaze, but he couldn't because I was looking down at my hands. Urban was crying. I heard him crying, and it tore at me because it was the last thing I wanted to give him, but it was all I had. The only thing that was true.

'We're going to help you want to live,' said Bengt.

'You don't realize it now, but there is a life for you, a good life, and it's waiting for you,' said Artan, and it was as if the entire room gasped because he had spoken for so long.

'Shall we agree, Anna, that you'll stay here for a while?'

I couldn't open my mouth. But I looked at Urban so he would understand that I refused. He had to do the greatest thing one person can do for another. He had to help me die.

'Then we're in agreement,' said Bengt, because he thought the meeting had lasted long enough.

All three stood up and held out their hands to me because I was supposed to shake them, but I couldn't. I couldn't have moved, if it hadn't been for Urban who had stuffed me into my down coat over my nightgown, and tied my boots. I had lifted my foot to help him. Maybe I had consented to it all? No. I had only done it because it was him. That was the only reason.

'Artan will show you to the ward.'

I looked at Urban, begged him with my eyes, but I saw that he was letting me go. That he was releasing me, to these three. To the entire hospital. That he had taken his hand from me and that he was going to rest now, because he had been carrying such weight.

I held him. Clung to him. I was screaming inside. But no one heard, so he left. He walked out the door after saying, 'I'll come and visit you. Every day at first.'

'It's best if you go now,' said Bengt. 'There's no point in dragging it out.'

The sound of the door. I was alone. I was more alone than I'd ever been, and I fell. Fell through my body, down to where the silence was with its yellow light around it like a wreath.

'Come on,' said Artan, lifting me off the floor, propping me up on my legs.

'Let's go,' he said then. 'One step, and then another. One foot in front of the other. Good.'

We walked down a hallway. Candy-striped sofas and small tables, numbers on the doors, into the room. A few people were sitting at one table, playing games. I couldn't look at them, but one woman with slanted bangs got up and stood in front of me.

'My name is Petra.' She looked through her papers. 'You're Anna; I'm working here tonight. Do you have any pets?'

Was Artan leaving? Who was this Petra? I fell down again, but Artan was quick and carried me the last few steps into the room.

'You're going to sleep in the therapy room tonight,' he said. 'The ward is full, but tomorrow you'll get a real room.'

Petra came in behind him, removed the telephone, and left. There was a small sofa bed, a table, and a piano too.

'It's late, so you'll get your dinner on a tray tonight. Otherwise we eat together, out there. It's an important part of treatment here. Goodbye, Anna. I'll come back tomorrow. Sleep well.'

He closed the door behind him.

I sat down on the small bed. Artan had left, and there was only one thought going through my head. *I can't be here. I can't be here.* I lay down on the bed and pulled the blanket over me. I did it even though I couldn't. I closed my eyes and it was crawling inside me and there was this pressure on my chest. Why didn't I die from it? It was like I had a giant's foot on my ribcage, pressing me down. I stared at the green fabric of the sofa bed until it grew dark and the colours disappeared and there was a knock at the door and Inga stepped in and she said that the Night had come. The Night, that was the night shift, I realized, because she had brought a tray of medicine. I was given both pills and some drops to swallow.

'So that you can sleep, dear, and it's also for the anxiety.'

The anxiety? What was the anxiety? I thought in the dark.

'Take it all, and try to think as little as possible to start with. You just have to believe that it will get better.'

I didn't say anything, but I swallowed everything she gave me. She left me alone, there in the bed, and I slowly felt the giant's foot disappearing, and something settled like cotton around my thoughts.

The morning came. I was awake. No. I was awake. The giant's foot was everywhere, coming in and pressing and leaving nothing behind. The light made its way into the small room. The window didn't have blinds; there was only a green curtain that covered the very top. What should I do? Where was Urban? The loss of him ripped and tore at me. And yet nothing would be better if he were here. I knew that the way you know that the sun will come up the next day. I was wearing a white nightgown with a blue logo on the chest. Every button was buttoned. When had that happened? Who had taken off my own nightgown and exchanged it for this one?

I sat on the window ledge to look at the sky, which was white and seemed full of snow that would soon fall. I didn't dare to go to the bathroom, even though I needed to. I couldn't leave this room, just as little as I could stay in it.

I sat there until there was a knock at the door and Artan stepped in.

'Good morning, Anna. Put on these clothes, now. I'll wait outside for two min-utes, and then I'll come back in.'

He left a white shirt and a pair of light-blue sweatpants, underpants, and a pair of socks; then he left again. I looked at the clothes he had left on the sofa bed. Couldn't do anything else. When Artan came in again, he looked at me and at the clothes and said that he would go get a female nurse if I didn't shape up.

'It's best for you to do it yourself. You might as well get dressed and get up for breakfast. I'll turn my back, and you put on your clothes.'

I did as he said. Why, I don't know; maybe because I thought of the woman with the slanted bangs, or Inga, whose voice in the dark scared me. I put on one article of clothing after another, until I was done. Then I sat down on the sofa bed, as if the effort it had taken to put on my clothes had taken all the strength I had left.

'Come on now,' said Artan. 'You can go to the bathroom and then you must eat breakfast.'

I needed to pee so badly that what came out of me never stopped. I sat there, feeling the water leave my body, and I thought, *there must not be anything left after that*, and I listened to the noise that didn't end, but finally it did after all. I avoided the mirror, just pulled up my underwear and my pants with my eyes on the red-speckled linoleum floor. The bathroom didn't lock, and I knocked on the door when I was finished to be let out. I didn't want to walk anywhere, so Artan held me up and led me to the breakfast table, where there were people sitting on almost all the chairs. I felt them looking at me, so I held firmly to my gaze so it wouldn't try to find anything. Artan had to press me into a chair and the surface of the table was worn; I could see that, at least. Artan got *filmjölk* and cornflakes and a cheese sandwich for me, and then he came back with juice and tea.

'Eat,' he said.

I lifted the spoon slowly and dipped it in the *filmjölk* and cornflakes and brought it to my mouth. Ate a bite. It stung my throat because I hadn't chewed the cornflakes. I did it again, but I tried to chew this time. Swallowed. It worked. One bite and then another one and all the time, Artan was there on the chair beside me like some kind of shield. The cheese sandwich tasted good. It was impossible to explain to myself why I ate the whole sandwich without difficulty. I drank up the juice, too, and tasted the tea.

'Good, Anna,' said Artan. 'The daytime medication will come soon, and then you'll take a shower.'

'No,' I said.

It just came out, that no. I didn't want to. I didn't want anything. I didn't want to be anywhere.

'It's better to shower than not to shower,' said Artan.

I looked at him, at his dark eyes, thinking about what they had seen. For one second I thought about it. Then it was just black again. As if I were closing myself off from the world that squeezed me and wanted to get into me. Everyone who was sitting around the table was staring at me. I could feel it, how their eyes were eating at me a little at a time.

I received a plastic cup with different-coloured pills and a bigger plastic cup with water to swallow them down. Artan held his hand above my shoulder and it was like it was saying *now you have to take your medicine and get better. You'll get better,* said the hand, *but it's going to take time. Do you have time, Anna? Do you have the patience it takes to get well? Are you strong enough,* the hand asked, and I didn't know anything, so I told the truth, that I knew nothing, but I took the medicine and washed it down with the water.

The minutes felt as long as years and I couldn't be in the sort of time that didn't move, that instead stood still and all I could think of was being allowed to die, being allowed to cut the thread of time forever. But first I had to shower. Artan spoke to me gently and firmly at the same time and he pushed me toward the shower room and once again he waited outside. The water washed over me. Hot, as hot as it could be without burning me, but it was impossible to get the water that hot. I washed my hair, and I didn't know when I had last done that; they had let me be, Urban, Ulf, Birgitta, and Sven. Just let me lie in bed and float through the days and nights, no difference between them. Birgitta had fed me, but that worked better with Urban, so in the end he had had to do everything, but he hadn't bathed me. And Birgitta probably hadn't dared to. I pumped out shampoo from a dispenser attached to the wall, and I ran my fingers through my matted hair, again and again until the mats loosened. I soaped my body with a bar of soap that was also attached to the wall. I washed my whole body, and I thought it was strange that I could do it even though I didn't want to. That I did as Artan said even though my entire being wanted to do otherwise.

Artan gave me an extra towel for my hair and I didn't do anything with it, so he dried my hair and together we walked to a supply room where I received a brush and another change of clothes.

'The best thing would be if you had your own clothes,' said Artan. 'But we'll worry about that later. Right now it's important for you to think only about this moment. Do you feel anything from the medicine?'

'No,' I said, and I wondered why I was lying to Artan.

Because, of course, I could feel something quieting inside me. I was lying because I didn't intend to stay here. I would go home and then I would find a way. A way that would present itself to me like a revelation.

'I'll show you where you're going to stay.

In room four; you'll share a room with Sara. She's just a little older than you and she's quite calm, so it should work out nicely.'

Artan led me into a room with pale-blue walls, and there were two beds there and one half of the room was bare, with just the bed and the nightstand and an empty wardrobe and the other half was sort of decked out with decorations: a moose and a stag, whose antlers had to hold this Sara's rings and jewellery, stood on the window-sill; there were drawings of a tree and a face with red cheeks and a blue mouth on the wall, and on the nightstand were piles of magazines.

I had to stay here? With someone else?

'No,' I screamed. 'No. No.'

I screamed and threw myself to the floor, beating my head against the floor until Artan grabbed me and held me, simultaneously backing up and pressing the alarm button. Suddenly the room was full of staff and I was given an injection and it was like being hit in the back of the head, or kicked is what I was, again and again.

I woke up because I couldn't move. I was strapped down and Urban was there.

'Anna,' he said. 'You have to believe. You mustn't do anything else.'

Artan was sitting in the room too. Why did the thought come to me that he looked tired?

'I brought chocolate and grapes,' said Urban. 'I want you to eat them and do as they say, do you hear me? Do it for my sake, if you can't do it for your own. I'm here, and I won't leave you. But you can't live at home right now. You're a danger to yourself.'

A danger to myself? Did Urban know something about the thread I was planning to break off? You never knew with Urban. I couldn't move, couldn't do anything but listen to what he was saying. There was something inside me that calmed down immediately and it wasn't like when they took away the giant's foot with the medicine; instead it was as if I found my footing.

Bengt, the senior physician, came into the room. It was clear that he was in a hurry, but he pretended that he wasn't. He sat down on a chair beside me.

'Anna, we can't have things this way. We don't want to restrain you, and you won't do anything like that again. You won't hurt yourself, you and I are going to agree to that right now. Right? Let each day follow the next, and don't worry about what you should do. You'll get better. We know that. You have to trust that. A period of depression always passes.'

A period of depression? Was that what I had?

'Anna, I'm going to take off the straps now, and then you're going to follow Artan and Urban to your room and you'll stay in there until it's time to eat.'

I felt Artan loosening the straps, first the ones across my arms, and then the ones across my hips and ankles. Urban helped me get up. I followed him into the room with the stag and the moose and I sat down on the bed.

Urban opened the box of chocolates and removed the gold paper from a Belgian praline and moved it toward my mouth. I opened my mouth and he placed the piece of chocolate on my tongue. I chewed it and felt the filling run down my throat with the chocolate. Together we ate one piece of chocolate after another. We didn't say anything to each other. We just chewed, swallowed, and ate, until the box was empty.

I lay in my bed, looking at the ceiling. A water stain unfolded like a flower and my thoughts were nowhere, because I had taken the medicine. Sara was lying in the other bed, paging through magazines, but I thought, *If I look at the water stain it will probably work.* It was snowing outside; I could see that, even though the windows were made of plastic so they couldn't be broken. Big, dry snowflakes fell from the sky and I didn't think about my skis or the family that would soon be eating dinner together, because I couldn't be there anymore. I hardly remembered how they moved around there, in that house. Birgitta and Sven and Ulf were so distant, as if they belonged to another life. Only Urban could move between the worlds. I pictured him before me. How he would row out to the island I imagined the hospital to be on. Maybe he had several lives, I thought, and I pictured the ferryman as he took Urban's hand to help him into the boat. Maybe Urban came here with death itself. Maybe he paid with his life, a little at a time, to come here. I had to ask him not to come, I thought, turning toward the wall. The textured wallpaper made the wall feel crumby, and I was blind and read it with my fingertips:

You shall die a death.
You shall die a quiet death.
You shall die a death.

'You're the girl who doesn't talk.' The voice tore a hole in the room. It was Sara with the stag antlers, and she was talking to me. 'Is there something wrong with your voice?'

I put my head under my pillow to keep her out. I can't be here. That was all I knew, but there was nothing in front of me, no path to walk on. The path ended on the island. It was the end of the line, and here I was. I squeezed my eyes shut and saw the colours move from yellow to orange and then red behind my eyelids. I fell down through a hatch and lay in the well along with the ancient well serpent. We would meet each other and look each other in the eye. I treaded water and waited for the slippery body, like a single muscle, which would come out of the deep in the well, and it would be decided who would live and who would die. Because I knew who I was. The doctor had asked and I hadn't been able to pronounce the name in that room with the plastic flowers, green with red berries, the vinyl chairs with the little table between them, so that you would know who was sitting where, who was healthy and who was crazy. Crazy? Was that what I was? No. No. Not like that. Not in that way. Was I sad, the doctor had asked. He noticed the flash at the word 'sad' because right away he leaned forward and asked what I was sad about.

I didn't answer. He didn't get anything out of me as we sat in his room with the typewriter and the little icon that hung on the wall. Was the senior physician a believer? Did he too believe in God's love like the congregation I couldn't think about? He had small, red, piggish eyes, I thought, and chapped skin. Dandruff rained onto his lapels, settling there like a white powder.

He leaned back and said, 'I know you can do it. You can speak and you will come to speak. Right now there is darkness around you, and it's as if you're living with your eyes closed, but you must let us carry the hope. We'll meet again in a week.'

In a week. Was I going to be here for an entire week, or even longer? Was this the second or third day? It felt like a whole life.

There, I felt the slippery body of the well serpent. So now we were going to meet. The serpent wound itself around me, pulling me down, and the serpent's eyes were green and we sank down to the bottom of the well, which was covered in brush and seaweed. We looked each other in the eye and it was like looking in a mirror. I saw myself at the instant I was born, I saw who I was without everything that had been placed upon me later, I saw my naked life; but it wasn't my father's eyes I was reflected in, it was the serpent's, and this was my last moment, the serpent told me, this is what death looks like, as quiet as a caress, as frank as a birth. I am going to kill you now, said the serpent, and I gave my consent. Kill me. Kill me.

Perhaps it was because I wanted it so much that the well serpent disappeared. Suddenly he was gone and I was lying in bed again, staring at the wall and listening to Sara.

'I'm going home soon. My mom misses me so much. It's driving her completely nuts and I feel well. The doctor says I'm stable. I know he and I aren't together anymore. I had trouble letting it go, you see. I like didn't accept that it was over. I had pictures of him on the wall here before, but I took them down with Micke. He helped me. Oh, Micke is in charge of my treatment. He sends me postcards sometimes when he's travelling. He's so great, Micke. Who's in charge of your treatment? Artan, right? He's really far too cute to work in a ward like this. It's kind of provocative. Don't you think?'

I stared at the water stain on the ceiling and tried to keep her out. The stag girl with the antlers and rings. Her blond hair and snub-nose. Her slippers that looked like bunnies. Artan wasn't there; you could sense it in the whole ward, whether he was there or not. If Artan had been there, he would have rolled in a screen so no one could see me.

I was still alive. Breathing in and out. It surprised me that life made room for itself there, far down in the darkness. That my heart continued to beat even though there was no room for it because the darkness surrounded it and held it in cupped hands. Hands which could close around its final beat at any moment. The darkness could do anything. So did that mean that there was a gleam of light somewhere inside me? Was it Urban? I would ask him to stop coming. I had to remember to tell him today. That it had to stop. He would understand. He would release me to the darkness if I asked him to. He would do what no one else could do.

There was a knock at the door and Sara's

mom stepped in, along with a nurse.

The mom was blonde like Sara, and she was wearing makeup. Her mouth was a red sea. She went over to Sara and embraced her. The nurse, whose name was Susanne, said that they would go to the therapy room and leave Anna alone. Sara looked at me triumphantly, as if to say that she had a visitor and she was loved and then they walked out of the room as a group and left me alone.

Alone. I was alone and at the word alone there was a twinge of pain; it plucked a string deep inside and I felt the pain before the tears came. The tears went with the hope, I knew, and I tried to beat them back again, the tears, back to where it was quiet inside me. I didn't want anything to do with tears.

There were a few grapes left on the nightstand, and I peeled one until only the flesh was left; then I carefully put it in my mouth and pressed it against my palate with my tongue so the grape fell apart in my mouth. I could do that. I could eat these grapes, although I wouldn't think about Urban, who had bought them and brought them with him. I would just eat one after the other. I peeled the grapes and placed their weary skins on the nightstand in a little pile and ate and ate. I ate the grapes until Sara came back. It was clear she'd been crying because she had black stripes under her eyes and her whole face was bloated. Her mom was nowhere in sight, but Susanne was with her and she sat down on the bed beside Sara and hugged her for a while.

Why did I feel sorry for Sara? Why had she found her way into me? I didn't want her there. Her homesickness and lovesick revelation.

Was it the light in me that embraced Sara?

I asked Susanne for a screen. Could I have one? 'Yes, maybe,' Susanne answered. 'I'll bring it up on rounds.'

*

There was breaded fish for dinner. Fish with potatoes and peas. I was still looking down at my plate and keeping the others out. The fish, with its greasy breading, tasted like almonds and butter. I mashed the potatoes in butter like I usually did at home. At home. Had I ever had a home? Wasn't I really just living in someone else's home? I wasn't like them, was I? We weren't like one another.

This was a thought I avoided more than all other thoughts. It was a thought I wasn't ready for, and I buried it as deeply as I could inside me, deep in the darkness. The question of my father.

Had he battled with the well serpent and taken the boat out to the island? Even though I knew that there was a road all the way here and that you just had to dump your prey in the waiting room like a piece of dead meat. A moose you had shot. I didn't ask myself that question. I mashed my peas and mixed them with the potatoes, chewed and swallowed. If I didn't eat I had to lie in bed with an IV, and this was still better than that. Susanne handed out *knäckebröd* sandwiches too. They crumbled between my teeth and were hard to swallow, but I washed them down with water. Swallowed and swallowed.

After dinner there was TV in the common room, or games down the hall, but I went straight to my room and lay on my bed. I was alone because Sara always watched TV. The sheets had stripes in different shades of blue, light and dark blue, and the pillowcase was snow-white and smelled good, like detergent. I stared at the rough wall and suddenly I missed my map of the Mediterranean.

My longing was like a sudden wave that slammed over me and I whirled around in its eddies under the surface. Torn here and there until I found the ground with my feet and I was walking on the bottom, I was running, until the next came. Yet another door to close. I closed it and shut my eyes. I didn't see anything behind my eyelids; it was all black and that's the way I wanted it. Being with the darkness that didn't say anything, didn't rip and tear, just let me sink, all the way to where the silence was like a grey sea, without waves, with a surface shiny like metal. I was bathing in that sea when there was another knock at the door.

It was Artan, who walked into the room without asking permission. He came in and sat on the bed.

'Tomorrow we're going to take a walk, you and I. We'll walk around the hospital park. I've asked Urban to bring clothes. It's cold out now,' said Artan.

I looked at Artan so he would understand that I couldn't. I couldn't move. I battled the well serpent and read the writing on the wall. I would die, just because I wanted to so much.

'It will just be you and me,' said Artan. 'It will be good. Do you want your evening snack in here?'

He brought a tray with tea and a cheese sandwich and I ate as he sat beside me on the bed.

'My dad died last night,' he said. 'We were all there, and he got to see his newborn granddaughter. We put her on his chest and he held her. A few minutes later he was dead.'

What did he say? His dad had died? Left

life and the others behind him in the room. Where had he gone? Had he stayed with them in the room and watched them close his eyes and place his hands together, or was he just gone? What had happened to Artan? His own father. Dead. He had taken the step across to the dead, where nothing existed, or was there something waiting for him there? Why was Artan here with me and not with his family? I tried to say something, pulling the strings that gathered my words, straightening out and separating.

'I'm sorry for your loss,' I finally whispered, but he heard me and he looked at me calmly and said thanks, and the tears I didn't want anything to do with came and they ran down my face; they streamed out because of this death with Artan and his wife and the little baby, who knew nothing of it of course, but who lay there on the dying man's chest as he drew his last breath and how his heart stopped like the pendulum of a clock, from one beat to another. Existing and not existing and Artan's face; he was crying too. The tears came and we cried together until our tears were gone and our breathing had calmed.

'Why are you here?' I asked.

'I need the money. Plus, I want to work.'

'Do you like it here?' I asked.

'Sometimes. I'm going to go now,' said Artan. 'Soon night will come and then it will be morning and then we'll go out for a walk.'

Artan left. I lay in the darkness, feeling the emptiness he had left behind. He had left emptiness and death behind him. I realized that everything I'd believed about death before was wrong. That death wasn't something you could ask for. It came to you, if you didn't seek it out yourself and throw yourself off a cliff or take too many pills. Then it would be there and shut off your heart the way you shut off the lights.

Artan's father was dead and I was alive. Artan was alive, and Urban. My father was alive. I counted the living and gathered them within me and the light that broke through embraced all the life that I had within me, even though I didn't want it to. There's not much you can do with the light and the darkness. They're there and they take up the space they're allowed. It's impossible to control the light and the darkness. Wasn't it strange that Artan's father's death spread light over me? Shouldn't it be the other way around?

I thought for a long time about how Artan was fatherless now. How he had had a father and now he didn't anymore. I couldn't understand it. Was it because I had a father myself and couldn't imagine a life without him, even though I had only seen him at my birth?

Night fell, and the medicine and ivs and Artan's father disappeared and I sank through my bed and anchored myself there. I lay perfectly still and looked out across the dark landscape. I saw the mountains and the stars hanging there and the sea taking its deep sighs over everything. I didn't want to move because then Urban would show up with his eyes and ask me to return to life, which I was no longer familiar with. The skis and the temperance, the congregation that scared me to my very core. I could never go back there. I'd rather listen to the sea and know nothing. I'd rather feel the wallpaper with its *die a death* until my breaths switched places with consciousness and sleep and I was carried out on the river, all alone, following its winding curves, and I broke up through the foaming water like a log that has torn itself loose.

It was the middle of the night when I awoke. I was very dizzy and my whole body was heavy, but I had to pee so I reeled toward the door and opened it. An aide, who was sitting and reading a magazine, stood up right away and grabbed me before I fell down and helped me to the bathroom. I peed and reflected on the fact that I was hungry. That it was the middle of the night and I was hungry. I wiped myself and held onto the sink so I could wash my hands. The aide met me outside the door and held onto me and started for my room. I resisted. No. No. I have to say I'm hungry, that I have to eat, but I couldn't so I ended up in bed again and the aide, I'd never seen him before, tucked me in and said good night.

I could probably manage it if I crawled, I thought, and I put both feet on the floor and started toward the door on all fours and then the aide was there again with his zeal for stopping me and I whispered, 'I'm hungry. Hungry,' so he could hear me.

He helped me to my feet and I leaned against him.

'Once is nothing,' he said, 'twice is habit. You can have the evening snack. Sit down. I'll give you a sandwich.'

Two more aides were sitting on a sofa, and they nodded at me and I realized that they wanted it to be quiet at night, so they could do other things. The aide brought a sandwich and milk and I ate it quickly and drank the milk.

'Okay then?' said the aide, pulling me up.

We walked toward room four together, and he dumped me in bed like a piece of meat, and I reflected on how I was just that.

Had I really taken that walk out into the ward in the middle of the night? Or had that been someone else? Was I Artan's father, wandering around, unable to decide if I should leave my family or not? The medicine pulled me down and I saw the colours darkening with every breath.

The spray of the shower woke me up; I stood under the water for a long time as it washed over and over me. They'd had to carry me out of the bed; this idea of taking a walk scared me more than anything else. It was about life, and I didn't want anything to do with that. Artan hadn't said anything about it today; he'd just carried me to the shower, but I knew he hadn't forgotten it even though his father was dead and everything. Urban must have brought clothes while I slept; maybe he didn't want to see me, maybe he saw that I was lost and would never come back. The giant's foot was there, tearing at me, but I hadn't received any medicine yet. Did I want medicine? It was always unsettling when the medicine cart came and the patients flocked like birds around the nurse, who always needed help from at least one aide to keep everyone back. They came in to me because I didn't get out of bed, but I could hear the ruckus out there and it scared me.

I turned off the shower, saw the steam on the mirror, and dried myself carefully with the towel. The medicine was waiting in my room and I gratefully took the little plastic bottle and swallowed the pills with the water the nurse had in a plastic carafe along with the cups. Soon the foot would disappear and my intestines would stop twisting. On the bed lay a pair of jeans, a yellow shirt, socks, a blue down coat, mittens, and a hat. I didn't want to look at the clothing, but it was there, waiting for me. Artan wouldn't give up.

I dressed in my usual clothes and brushed my hair until the mats were gone. I put my hair up in a ponytail and I thought, *maybe I look normal, but none of this is for real.* I was dressed as myself, but I was somewhere totally different.

I looked down at the floor as I walked to the breakfast table. I had never spoken to any of the patients, not even Sara, even though she talked to me sometimes of course, asked me to tell her which looked best on her: this headband or this one;

what did I think about lipstick, didn't dark lips make you look old?

I ate and I knew that Artan was there in the background somewhere. I had difficulty swallowing, and the tears threatened to come, so I swallowed and swallowed and finally my food was gone and I felt Artan's hand on my shoulder.

I cried with my hat on, and my coat in the way. Artan bent down and tied my boots. Then he looked me in the eye and said, 'Let's go now. You and I. Just a little walk in the park.'

I thought it was strange that he could take a walk with me now when he really ought to be at home, and it felt unfair toward him. I cried because I didn't dare to do it.

'I can't do it, Artan. I can't do it.'

My nose was running and I cried and sobbed, but all along I knew inside that I couldn't get out of it. That nothing could stop what was about to happen.

'Let's go now,' said Artan.

He took me by the arm, his hand at my elbow, and held me up, firmly; there was no hesitation in Artan.

We walked out through the locked door; Artan opened it with his key and then locked it again. The stairwell smelled like old snow. We took the few steps toward the elevator and Artan nudged me into it. There were mirrors everywhere, and I caught sight of the one of us two who was me, and it was a sight that made me shout.

'No. No.'

I hit him, but he took my hands in his at once and looked at me gravely.

'You don't hit me. Do you hear me? Never.'

The elevator door opened, and it led out to the doorway, a steel door in the middle of the yellow-painted stairwell. A rubber mat lay there, with slush on it, and that was probably what smelled, along with the snow that was outside. Artan was still holding me by the elbow, and he gave me a little push out.

'There we go. One step. Another step. You can do it. Good.'

I walked beside him. I was walking on a sanded path, and the ice under it was grey. There were snowbanks beside me because someone had shovelled. The park was covered in white, and we walked there, Artan and I. I smelled the dry snow and the bright sun melting it. I tried to look down at the ground, but Artan kept saying, 'Look at the birds! Do you see that bush?' And then, 'Turn around, and you can see the hospital.'

I turned around and saw the red-and-white multistorey building. It looked like a little castle.

'That's where you are now, but it won't be forever. You're going to get well.'

'Am I sick now?' I asked, because I thought I might need to know.

'Yes, right now you're sick. You are depressed.'

'Is that wanting to die?'

'Yes. That too,' said Artan before he turned me away from the hospital so I could see the hill down to the kiosk and the road next to it.

I couldn't manage any more. How long had we been out? Five minutes?

'Artan,' I said. 'We have to go in now.'

'Feel the snow first,' he said, but I refused.

He couldn't make me. I couldn't do it. I knew that my refusal was stronger than his will.

'No. I can't. I can't!' I shouted in his face and he looked at me and I could see what he was thinking.

'That's enough for today. But tomorrow we'll come out again.'

He held tight to me, as if he were afraid of dropping me, and this time I closed my eyes as we got on the elevator. All the way up, and then he had to lead me out and when he rang the bell to get into the ward I opened my eyes again, but I just looked at my shoes and the puddles forming under them as the snow melted.

*

It was an exhaustion that crowded out everything else, and I slept all day. When I woke up there was a tray of food on a rolling table, and I ate the chicken and potatoes without posing a single question to myself. *What did the food taste like? Where was I?* I didn't know. I just brought the fork to my mouth, again and again. Artan had left, and Urban hadn't been there. It was just me and the room, holding me in its grip. The screen someone had put up because I'd asked for it scared me with its frosted surface. I didn't want it there, but I couldn't tell anyone. Not now. Not when the last glimmer of light had disappeared. I had a headache and it was bursting behind my eyes, as if they wanted out of my head, out of their sockets. I saw my eyes carried away on a plate to be put in some other head. I saw it happen and I couldn't do anything because my tongue was paralyzed and my throat was torn to shreds. I felt inside my eye sockets and it was so soft in there and wet and the blood ran down my hands and arms.

'Anna.'

It was Sara; had she been lying there all this time?

'Anna, are you awake? I'm going home, Anna. I'm going home tomorrow. The doctors said so. My mom was so happy, Anna, I talked to her on the phone and everything is still where I left it. Everything.

'Anna, I'm going to miss you. Well, every-one. They're all so nice here. Aren't they? Anna, you never say anything, but I know you wish me well.'

I was forced to think about Sara, lying there in her bed, and her longing, but I didn't have room for it, she was so big.

I swept my arm to silence her and she didn't say any more. I didn't know why I knew that it wasn't true, what she had said, but I knew it. That her mom wanted her to be here; I had seen it in her mouth, the red sea that opened and closed.

I felt *You shall die* with my fingers on the wall and it calmed me to know that that was how it would end. The life I had no idea how to live. The life that went on out there, that I had been a part of.

There was a knock at the door and there was Urban. He smelled like snow and sweat, he had been at practice; he had his bag with him. He stood in the crack of the door with the light behind him.

'Anna,' said an aide named Per Ola. 'Go sit in the therapy room, you and your brother, so Sara can be alone; she's sad tonight, Sara is.'

I followed Urban out into the light. I followed him into the small room where I'd slept the first night. I followed the scent of snow and warmth he spread around him. We sat down on the little sofa bed and he opened his bag and took out a chocolate bar. He broke off a piece and gave it to me and I ate and let the chocolate run out of my mouth and onto my chin, so Urban left me alone in there and went to the bathroom and got paper towels to wipe me with. He said nothing at first, and I couldn't say anything either, and I wondered if my eyes were where they belonged as I felt the tearing in my throat.

'Anna. I have a letter from the family. The nurse has it. They thought it was too much for you right now. You mustn't be afraid, Anna.'

You mustn't be afraid, Anna echoed through me. Was that what I was? Urban ought to know, right? I couldn't think about how things were at home, so I looked at Urban's mouth, how carefully he formed his words. *You mustn't be afraid, Anna* bounced between the walls and I could feel my heart running riot in my chest. When could I ask the question? If he could help me die? No, I had to manage it on my own, I had to find a way. I realized now that it wasn't about wanting to, not entirely, and as long as I was in here I wouldn't die. Maybe that was the whole point of my being here?

When the chocolate was gone Urban would leave. I saved a bit in my hand until it melted and got sticky and I ate it off my hand with my teeth, making lines in the chocolate.

'I heard you went outside today,' said Urban.

I stared at him. Did he know that? What else did he know?

'That's good,' he said. 'That's really good.'

I could tell that he wanted to say something about the skis, but he didn't let himself. It was like he took a breath, as if to prepare himself, but he changed his mind and the image of skis appeared in that empty space, like a picture from another life.

'Have a nice time now, Anna,' he said, hugging me, but I couldn't hug back because now this moment was over and he was going to leave me to the loneliness in here, and it was impossible to stay in it. It was like I tiptoed around this ward and that was the only way it could be.

I was deep inside the softness that settled around my thoughts when I suddenly sat up. It was night, and the moon was hanging in the sky and looking down on me with its white glow. I had been dreaming; I had eaten gravel and my mouth was bleeding and was it doing that for real? I felt in my mouth, but there was nothing there, just spit, and I felt down so far that it felt like I was going to throw up. I had sand in my mouth, I could feel it, and yet I didn't. I had to rinse my mouth. I was unsteady on my feet, but I held onto the wall and the night staff looked in my direction, and Pär, a tall man with dark hair, came to help but I waved him off to show that I could take care of myself. I took the couple of steps to the bathroom and to be safe I didn't turn on the light. I rinsed and rinsed my mouth clean and it was as if the sand was stuck in my teeth, scraping, but that was impossible of course, I told myself, and I kept rinsing until my mouth didn't squeak anymore and I turned off the tap and felt for the door handle in the darkness, but it wasn't there; the handle was a knife and I cut my hand and the blood flowed, streaming down onto the floor. I felt the warm blood leaving me and I had to grasp the knife a second time to get out of the bathroom. The night staff ran to me, carried me into a room where the nurse came and bandaged me. 'How was it possible?' they said. For me to have a knife on the ward. Where was the knife? The nurse cleaned and put on compresses and pressed and pressed against the blood that kept coming through the compresses so she had to keep changing them.

Finally they controlled the bleeding and my hand was in a tight bandage. Who had given me the knife? Was it Urban, I heard Pär ask. And then a heap of words rained down over me: rounds, suicidal, inadequate procedures. They brought me back to my room, laid me on my bed, and brought extra IVs, and Pär sat on a chair in the room and looked at me in the dark. His eyes were like two black holes and I rolled over on my side so I was lying against the wall, because I didn't want him there. He was like an animal waiting to pounce on me.

Bengt's face was the first thing I saw when I woke up. I saw his red piggish eyes looking down at me and he had a beret on his head, and a coat. He must have come straight here, without first taking off his outerwear in his room with the icon and the dried flowers.

'We're going to have a talk, you and I. They'll come get you at ten o'clock. Until then I want you to do what you normally do. Medicine, breakfast, but you can't shower today. We need to take care of your cut.'

I thought about how it was the cut they wanted to take care of, not me. If they'd been taking care of me, I never would have ended up here, and Urban popped into my mind. His way of saying 'You should be here. Trust me.'

The patients were sitting over there at the

breakfast table like a cluster that moved according to a given pattern, and I walked over to them with Pär only a step behind. Get breakfast, chew, lean toward one another, and look down at the plate. It was like a dance, with everyone's small movements creating one large, billowing movement. A movement everyone took part in, each in his or her own way. It struck me that even my refusal was part of this larger whole, that I sat there like a fundamental tone, refusing to see. I took some food and it was hard now that my hand was bandaged, so Petra helped me, the woman with the slanted bangs and the pets. I shovelled down my cornflakes with one hand; the other lay helplessly on the table. I was given a sandwich and I ate it like I usually did. Petra took my plate and put it on the kitchen cart and then she took me by the arm to help me up, even though I could do it myself.

Petra followed me to my room, just a few steps behind me, and I became frightened of having her there behind me. What was this? Why couldn't I be by myself as usual?

There were clothes on the bed, my own, Urban had brought them and I realized that I was supposed to get dressed with Petra in the room. I put things on as best I could, but Petra had to help me and pull open the shirtsleeve so my bandaged hand could get through.

We walked down the hallway, out through the ward, and across to the other side where the doctors sat in their rooms, typing on their typewriters or speaking into their Dictaphones. And they were talking about us; I knew that now. Petra knocked on Bengt's door and he opened it right away, as if he had been standing by the door waiting for us.

'Sit down, Anna. Petra, you can wait outside,' he said, and his beret was hanging on the coat rack along with his coat and his chapped head was red under his hair. I sat down in an easy chair and Bengt took his chair and set it down right across from me as if he didn't want the desk to be in the way now that we were going to talk to each other.

'Anna, where did the knife come from?' He searched for my gaze, which wanted to wander to the icon and to the window, but he caught me with his small eyes and I realized I would have to answer. I fought with my throat to get control of the words that were all mixed up down there.

'It was the handle,' I said, although I knew this was the wrong answer.

'Did Urban bring the knife?' he asked me then.

I looked out at him, trying to understand who he was. If he knew about the well serpent and the gravel, if he knew how the moon shone. But even though he was a senior physician here, he knew nothing, and that scared me so much my heart beat in my chest.

'No,' I said.

I tried, anyway, to say that no, but it didn't come out into the room; it just lay inside my mouth.

'No, no.' I tried hard to get that no out. 'No, it wasn't Urban.'

'Anna. What happened? We have strict procedures here, you see. Every patient is searched when they arrive. The kitchen knives are locked up and no sharp objects are allowed in the ward. So I'm asking you again. Where did the knife come from?'

'It was the door handle,' I said again.

That was all I could say. That was more than I could say. I remembered the night that had passed and the handle burning in my hand, the blood flowing out of me.

'Anna. We have to put an extra watch on you now that we know you have self-harming behaviours. You will always have someone with you. You may not use the bathroom on your own. Someone will sit by your bed when you're sleeping. But you must tell me where the knife came from. Did you go into the kitchen when they were preparing dinner?'

I shook my head. I hadn't.

'You and Artan took a walk. Did you take anything from Artan?'

I shook my head again.

'I notice that we're not getting any further, Anna. We'll have to increase your medication. I believe you have delusions. That you don't remember. The medicine will help you sort out your thoughts and it will keep you calm. Do you understand what I'm saying?'

'I don't want to.'

The words fell out of me and landed in his lap and I clearly saw him pick them up one by one and polish them the way you might polish an apple.

'Then that's settled, Anna,' he said with the apples in his hands. 'And I'll bring up the inadequate procedures with the staff.'

He patted me on the shoulder.

'It wasn't your fault that it happened.'

I was swimming underwater. Stroke after stroke. Bells were ringing and the congregation was sitting on chairs in rows on the bottom and their folded hands were white and their hair billowed in the water. Erik was at the very front with his hands extended. 'We pray to the living God,' he sang. I swam toward them, toward the clocks, toward their outstretched hands. 'We sing praises to the living God,' Erik sang, and I swam to an empty chair that was set apart from the others. I sat down on it and held myself in place so I wouldn't float up. The congregation turned to me as I sat there and their song became stronger. They were screaming. Screaming with wide-open mouths and their mouths were like the screams. Unbearable. I let go of my chair, but I didn't float up. I was stuck. They looked at me with their eyes and I felt my heartbeat and I tried to escape, but I was theirs. I belonged to them more than I could ever believe, and I screamed too. My scream made them stop and Anna-Lisa turned to me, slid down into my lap, and held her hand over my mouth. I tried to get away; I pulled her long hair and then I hit her in the face, tore at her with my nails until she was bleeding, but she wouldn't let go. I couldn't breathe and my vision was going black and I felt death like a black shadow before I fell. I fell down into the blackness and I heard the congregation's prayers from a distance, prayers to save my soul, which God would receive as one of his own. I cried, cried because it was over, because I hadn't been able to do more, because life as I knew it was over.

Artan looked at me and I could see that he was disappointed. He didn't say anything, but I could see in his shoulders that he was measuring a distance between us. There had always been a distance, but it had grown larger. He was sitting on a chair in my room and he had a book, and I lay there looking at the flower on the ceiling, which unfurled so slowly that you couldn't see it. I was ashamed because he was sitting there and because I didn't do anything. Would he sit there and watch me just lying there? It felt as if I were nothing and as if he had to watch over this nothing. I was ashamed that this was a part of his life. That I took up his time. I felt like I had to say something to him and I tried to find the right words and finally I said, 'I don't want this.'

'No,' said Artan. 'I know. You never should have cut yourself, Anna.'

Could Artan understand? No. No one could understand.

'No,' I said.

Artan continued to read his book and he tapped his feet, irritated, but he couldn't say anything to me. Not now. I had let him down, his tapping feet tried to say, *you didn't just let yourself down, you let me down too. I believed in you, Anna*, he said with his feet. *We were on the right track, but we aren't anymore.* I realized that an aide should never expect anything of a patient, never invest anything of himself in the person he cares for, and maybe Artan had done that, without realizing it himself.

I sank through the layers, just let it happen, because it was too painful to be awake. I met the ferryman, who invited me aboard, but I kept going to the stag girl who was sitting on a bench and crying, and on to the shining day, where the light was so bright that it was impossible to see. I felt my way with my hand and went into the light, onto the street with the house with the family, who were all sitting inside eating food. I entered the house without anyone noticing me and I went into my room, where the map was, and I thought, *now that I've seen it I'll remember it for always.* I turned to the nightstand with the letters and they were there and the sight of them caused me to back out of the room and disappear from the house and go through the light back to my body where my pelvis lay anchored in the bed.

*

The new medicine made my tongue stiff and if I hadn't been able to talk before, it was impossible now. I slurred out the words *yes, thanks, no* to the staff's questions about whether I wanted to shower, whether I wanted another sandwich. My hand had healed and there was just a red mark there now, and it itched. My body was rigid; it had frozen stiff from the inside out and I felt like an iced-over lake, with room only for my lungs pulling the air in and out and for the fist which was my heart, which kept on beating deep inside the frozenness.

I was banned from having visitors. I thought about Urban. About whether he might be relieved. I didn't know what it cost him to visit me. Maybe he was glad to be spared it. I understood. I wouldn't have wanted to visit myself. Maybe it was just as well that I was left here, because I would never get away. That's what I thought now. Death seemed distant. As if it didn't belong to me anymore, as if it weren't a possibility. I saw it only in my dreams, and I approached it. It was the ferryman, and the singing mist, or the gravel pit that was waiting to fall. The dog with the red eyes. I always recognized it, no matter what it looked like, but I never got close enough.

I wondered about my will. My will to live? Did it exist anywhere? What could a life look like? What would happen to me? Would I be pushed out to the table where they played games? Would I get to start taking walks again? Artan didn't say anything about that. He didn't say anything, he just helped me with what was most necessary. I sat on the window ledge during the day, fantasizing, with him or someone else in the room. Somehow I had grown used to always having someone there, even when I went to the toilet, even if the shame was always there. To always having a witness to this refusal, this non-life that had been going on for a long time, I don't know how long.

I stroked the plastic window with my hand. I saw the spring out there, and the dandelions finding their way up out of the snow. I felt inside what the ground smelled like: wet, warm snow and the ground underneath. I thought of the river breaking loose and making room for itself, of lined rubber boots that itched, and I understood, of course, that these thoughts belonged to life. Should I tell Bengt about the river?

Should I tell Artan?

Artan was reading peacefully in his chair. It looked like he was concentrating. I wondered what book he was reading. Could I ask him that?

'Artan,' I said with my tongue in the way, so I sounded like an old man. 'I want to go outside.'

Artan looked up from his book. He looked at me, as though he were trying to figure out who I was. What I wanted. That voice I had.

'That won't be easy,' was all he said, and he kept reading his book, as if he were refusing me access, as if the path into him was closed. I knocked and knocked at that door. I saw myself doing it. I almost hit him, but he just sat there in my room, like a statue, I thought, and I didn't try using my voice again because the daytime medication was coming on the cart and Sonja was the one bringing it. The one with the skinny arms, so you could clearly see the bones underneath. She nodded at Artan and then looked at me.

'Come down from the window,' she said. 'Sit on the bed; I'm going to draw blood.'

I did as she said, helping by lifting my arm so she could tie the band around it. She patted me on the inside of my elbow and smiled encouragingly.

'Nice veins. Not everyone is so easy to stick.'

It was as if she were complimenting me because my blood stood out so clearly in my veins, and I watched as she stuck me with the needle, how it moved in under my skin. She changed tube after tube. She wiggled them up and down and placed them in a little stand she had on the cart. Then she gave me the medicine and I swallowed it with water and opened my mouth wide to show that I hadn't hidden any pills in there.

'Thank you, Anna,' Sonja said, and she went away again after she'd nodded at Artan again.

The door closed behind her and the room waited out the sound and then settled back to normal again. It was half dusk by now, and surely he couldn't read in that light, I thought.

'You won't have to have the extra guard tomorrow,' Artan said suddenly. His voice filled the whole room, coming to rest all the way up at the ceiling and falling back down.

'Good,' I said, and after this conversation it was like we were drained of all our strength and I realized that it took effort to sit so motionlessly on a chair, even if he did have the book.

Artan took another breath and forced it out: 'I'm going soon, and then Rodney will come, okay?'

'Okay,' I said.

There was nothing wrong with Rodney. He was one of the ones who would bring extra sandwiches before night fell. We sat in the dark for a long time, and I knew that Artan was only pretending to read. Had he been pretending all along? There had been some talk that I would be allowed to read the family's letter, but it wasn't time yet, but maybe soon? I wanted Urban to be with me, or at least Artan. Maybe I couldn't read anymore. The new stiffness in me pulled me in two. It was as if I had two sides that were pulling away from each other. I walked poorly, seeming to sway this way and that toward the breakfast table. Maybe the stiffness would pull apart the words that were written on the paper, like they did when I spoke. I hadn't read anything since I came here, or written anything either.

Rodney knocked on the door and stuck his head in, and Artan stood up, relieved. It was clear they liked each other, because they shook hands and smiled at each other so their teeth gleamed in the darkness.

'How are things here, then?' Rodney asked.

'Nice and quiet,' said Artan, and then, 'Are you coming to the party?'

'Yes,' said Rodney, laughing. 'Hell yes. Anything could happen.'

Artan laughed too.

'See you there, then,' said Artan, and he left the room without saying goodbye.

'Do you want it this dark, or can I turn on a light?' Rodney asked, and when I didn't say anything he turned on the overhead light.

'Do you want to borrow a magazine?' he asked.

I shook my head.

'Do you just want to sit there?'

I got my voice ready, tried to sneak past my tongue, and said, 'I can't talk.'

'Poor you, Anna,' Rodney said, and why did he say that, because his words brought tears and they ran and ran down my cheeks. The tears that had lain there, frozen solid and secure, now they were surging out of the deep like an army, and I cried and my nose ran as I sat there hating myself for these tears. The tears kicked their way out. They were impossible to stop. They made their way past the stiffness as if it were nothing, and out into the light where I sat with Rodney, who was beside me now. He seemed to embrace all of me, although he was only holding my shoulder.

'It's good,' said Rodney. 'It's good that you're crying.'

I walked straight out of the room with Rodney behind me; I started running down the hall up to the door of the common room, which was open, and then I turned around and ran back, but there was no place to run for real. I felt my muscles tightening around the movement and helping me on, step by step, as if they had just been waiting for this chance to stretch out, but I was caught by Rodney, who was holding me tight from behind and I cried and cried, screaming and crying until I fell to my knees and vomited. It was as if I were vomiting out my entire being there on the floor; the tremors came through my body and pulled back like waves. It was like they would never end, but finally the waves stopped coming and Rodney helped me to the bathroom, where I rinsed my mouth and my face with cold water; I got my shirt and pants wet, but I didn't care, and with

Rodney's help I made it back to my bed. He laid me down carefully as if I were a small child being put to bed, and his hand was cool on my forehead. He sat down on the chair right next to the head of the bed and for some reason I happened to think about Sara who was always sitting in the common room with the TV and the others. About how she never got to go home, but I couldn't explain why I was thinking about her right then. I was glad that Rodney was sitting there. I was scared. It was as if something was showing itself to me, as if something had been decided, but I didn't know what.

Meaning. Meaning. I woke up with the words aching in my chest. I opened my eyes and looked around at the room I hated. The clothes on the floor; the dust, sharply outlined by the light, which I had done all I could to keep out. I closed my eyes again. My thoughts were moving through it like sluggish snakes: *don't want to. Not this. Never again*. I curled into a foetal position and rocked myself to keep the thoughts at bay.

What would I do? I had to get the day to turn to night. Unconsciousness was the only thing I looked forward to. Sleep was liberation. For some reason, my dreams were bright.

Sleep had inscribed my face during the night. Red grooves of hopelessness that would disappear imperceptibly during the day. Everything was stiff and frozen solid inside me. *To get to die. To get to die*, echoed through me. And at the same time, this hunger. Why? Oh, how I hated myself and what I had become without noticing. Day by day, week by week, I had created this monster that was myself.

If only I could fall asleep again. I pressed my face into my pillow, pulled the blanket over myself, and wondered when the medicine would come. It was a blessing to follow my breath in and out as I walked through the tunnel that always burned with light at the edges. *Oh, that light*, was the last thing I thought before I fell asleep again.

When I woke once more, it was evening and Urban was in the room. Urban's goal of never despising anyone got on my nerves, while at the same time it amazed me, and I knew that he had a sort of knowledge that I myself completely lacked. My own gaze was merciless and cruel, while Urban looked at me with no judgment. Urban didn't judge anyone. He was at ease in himself. His perspective and ability to measure time was intact. When had I lost that ability?

I had memories. Of course I had those. I remembered the sea. I remembered the sky. The sky and the sea. I remembered my father.

Wait. I remembered the gifts I had received as a child.

Get up! Get up! Urban ought to shake me, hit me with those hands he had. Instead he gave me grapes and chocolate as I lay there. The way you'd feed a dog. But the day had gone by unnoticed. That made me calm. The pressure on my chest eased. I scooted up until I was sitting. I looked at the door that closed me in. That kept the world out. The wood had grown worn with time and it was dotted with ingrained grime. The walls propped one another up. Kept the room in place. Apparently unaware of me. The sound from the ward bothered me. My hearing was so sensitive that I could hear the TV from the common room, could hear them talking to each other, could hear when someone threw dice. I was crying again. Why couldn't I die? Why wouldn't jumping from the window lead to liberation?

Eternity. Isn't that word terrifying? To get to die. To get to die. To go from life to the great, silent room where death was. To feel the last beat of my heart. I was denied this liberation. Why?

Because I was Athena.

There was a rush through the pipes in the room. I listened to the sound, heard someone flushing a toilet. Urban was still sitting by the bed, but soon he would leave and I would once again be on my own. I avoided the word 'alone' because I knew it could bring tears. Instead I concentrated on the sound of the pipes. I closed my eyes and imagined that it was my own brain, being washed clean. All the winding paths I had soiled with my incompetence. I was cold, and I put on a big knitted sweater, which was on the floor next to the bed. If only they would bring the medicine. I had used up my sleep during the day. I knew inside me that it would be a sleepless night, and I shuddered. What would I do with all that time? All the hours inexorably following one another? I took one of the chocolate bars, opened it, and ate it. I couldn't stop eating once I'd started. I took bite after bite. I hardly chewed; I just swallowed and felt the sharp corners tear at my throat. I swallowed it down with the water that was in the plastic carafe on the nightstand, and something grew quiet. My anxiety?

It had been a long time since I had wanted to understand things. How one thing led to another. There were a number of questions I was avoiding. Ones I had to avoid. I closed my eyes again to keep them out. Sometimes they would throw themselves over me with a strength I couldn't defend myself against with anything other than the medicine, but for the most part, they hibernated inside me and that's the way I liked it.

I tried to preserve this stillness. I reflected that now is now and there isn't anything else. There was a voice inside me that stubbornly told me that this wouldn't work any longer. It wouldn't work.

'They're going to let you start taking walks again,' said Urban. 'I've talked to Bengt and Artan, and they think it's a good idea too.'

I didn't want to. I didn't want to do anything, not even listen to Urban talking, so I turned away from him and looked at the textured wallpaper.

'We all agree that you have to get up and about more. You'll have to force yourself at first, but it will get easier. I know you don't understand that now, but it will get better and you will too.

'I'd like to read you the letter from the family, may I?' At the word 'family,' the tears came again. *Family, alone, father*; those were the words I avoided and now he was there with his hands, ripping and tearing at me. He kept a steady grip on my longing, and he didn't understand that this wouldn't work.

'No, Urban,' I said to the wall. 'Go away now.' When he didn't get up, everything turned black inside me and I flew at him and held his head in my hands and screamed, 'Go now. Go.'

But Urban was stronger; he took my arms and loosened my grip.

'Don't think you can scare me. Don't ever think that. Lie down. I know it by heart.'

He started speaking, his voice ringing out into the room, so loud as if to drown out my thoughts.

'Dearest Anna! We think about you every day, about how you're there and we're here and about how we want so much for you to come back to us. We love you, you see. We love you as if you were one of us. You are one of us and you have been since the first day we came and got you. You mustn't be afraid or in despair. You just have to stay where you are and with every day you will get better, and when you're ready you will come home to us. Your room is waiting for you. We're cleaning it and keeping it nice. Putting flowers on your nightstand. We miss you all the time. Maybe you don't believe it now, but there is a life for you here with us. We love you. Sven, Birgitta, Ulf, and Urban.'

We love you.

We love you; it went around in my head and mixed with my thoughts. Was I still going to be allowed to go back there? Was there a way back?

This time I dressed myself. Long johns under my jeans, an undershirt, the knitted sweater, and my down coat, hat, and mittens. Artan's 'it's pretty warm out' ran right off of me. For me it was winter, like the last time we were outside. Artan unlocked the door and then closed it behind us. My heart pounded in my chest as we approached the sliding doors.

There was only snow here and there; the ground was mostly bare, and I walked in the wet, flattened grass, arm in arm with

Artan. The air was whining with all the little birds calling out, and it was a sound I had to keep out, so I pulled down my hat. The bolted-down outdoor furniture stood here and there in the hospital park, so you could sit down somewhere and enjoy the weather or a cup of coffee.

'I thought we would take the path by the water,' said Artan. 'It's a slightly longer walk, but I believe in wearing you out.'

I didn't say anything to that; I just walked beside him, surrounded by all this life, feeling like a stranger, like something from another time. We walked around the lake, which was still frozen in spots; the small boats were pulled up, upside down on wooden sawhorses, and the owners were there, making sure everything was all right, with their thermoses and oranges.

Artan was walking quickly, his arm linked with mine.

'Walk, Anna. Walk faster.'

I did as he said and it was like we were flying over the path and around the lake. *Who is Artan?* I asked myself, *that he can fly like this?* We encountered people who were out walking their dogs, or just taking a walk, and I blinked at the light, which danced like blue spots behind my eyelids every time I closed my eyes. But Artan was quick with his 'Look, Anna. Look at that boat, how beautiful it is, painted red and blue,' and I saw, of course. I saw it all. All of it, I saw. The orange orange peels, the man's eyes as he watched us flying there, the childish blue watery colour of the sky, the scents of the ground, which seemed to be steaming there at our feet. Artan sped up and I followed him, as if I were stretching myself after him, because now he didn't care whether I came with him. I fought with my whole being to keep up with his pace.

When we landed in the hospital park again, he said, 'We missed lunch. I'll think of something.'

Steam came off me as I entered the ward, and I didn't want anyone to see it so I hurried into my room and quickly hung my coat in the wardrobe and I just tossed everything else in and closed the door. I threw myself down under the blanket and felt my heart gradually start to beat more slowly. I closed my eyes and the colours behind my eyelids were so bright that they hurt.

Did I want this? Did I want this light? I had no answer, and the questions that arose piled up and tangled up like threads inside me. Artan's face popped up, first as shadow, and then he appeared for real with his dark eyes and he was carrying a tray. Oh, how I hated these trays, I thought. All the plastic carafes and the soap that was attached to the wall. Oh, how I hated this ward with its fixed times and its particular rhythm that was impossible to slide into.

And yet I wouldn't go home. I was sure of that. Sure that that time had passed and could never return. I knew nothing about my future, and this severed tie was what I held in my hands.

Was that why I couldn't get well? No matter how much I liked Urban, we wouldn't be siblings. Birgitta and Sven and Ulf, they were far behind me and I had travelled on a path they couldn't tread. There was no way back. Did Urban know that? Deep inside?

'Boiled cod, potatoes, and peas,' said Artan, placing the tray on the nightstand.

I ate it all, shovelling it down as if I'd never eaten before. *Like a dog*, I thought, and I was ashamed for Artan to see me like this. But he didn't say anything; he just sat there on his chair, waiting for me to finish. When he would eat, I didn't know.

'We'll keep taking our walks,' was all he said, and he left with the tray.

The stiffness was something I had grown used to. That my body went in different directions. And my thoughts. It was like jumping from one ice floe to the next, with a crevice of cold sea between them. I had found a way to control my tongue, if I had to say anything. Which almost never happened. I didn't even speak to Artan very much—only the simplest things, the things that were necessary for us to go out. I answered when spoken to, but no more than that. But the light that had made its way in was always there in the dark, and I didn't want to call it by its true name, but sometimes on my own, in the dark, before I went to sleep, in the embrace of the medicine, I spelled out the word 'hope.'

*

'The walks are helping you get better,' said Bengt. 'It's good that you're accomplishing them. As I understand it, they're something you look forward to. I would like you to be more active in the ward too. Participate in something, Anna, even if it's just watching TV after dinner. You don't have to interact with the other patients at all. It's fine if you stick to the aides. But force yourself to do something. Play a game. Can we agree on that, Anna? That you'll play a game next time? I'll tell one of the aides on the ward.'

I didn't say anything. A game? What was he talking about? I was supposed to play a game? Bengt had on a white shirt with pale-blue buttons, and the wobbly intern was there too, and he nodded encouragingly at me and I thought he smelled like alcohol, so I said that, 'you smell like alcohol,' and he said, 'what do you know about alcohol, Anna?' 'That it's a curse,' I said, and at that word, curse, he wrote something down on his notepad.

'Curse, that's a strong word, Anna.'

As if there were strong and weak words, and he leaned toward me and I asked what a weak word was, but he didn't answer; he just leaned back again and ran his hand through his hair. He did that several times, until Bengt said, 'Then we have an agreement. I'll tell Rodney; he's coming tonight.'

We sat out in the hall and it felt threatening, with everyone who might go by; I had still only looked at Sara, and the others were like shadows flitting by. I was afraid of them, it was as simple as that. That we were alike, and that I would see that likeness if I looked at them. I had never sat on the candy-striped sofa before; I'd only seen it out of the corner of my eye.

'This is Yahtzee,' said Rodney, trying to catch my eye. 'There are five dice, and you have to collect different things. Just roll the dice and I'll explain it as we go.'

He gave me the dice and I took them, of course; I held them in my hand.

'Throw them on the table,' said Rodney. 'You can do it.'

I threw the dice on the table. The sound when they landed on the surface of the table.

'Look here. You have two fives. Save those and roll the other dice again. You're going to collect fives,' he explained.

I threw them again. 'Skritch,' it sounded in my head.

'There, another five. Good. Roll again.'

I took the two dice and tossed them out on the table. A four and a three.

'Fifteen for three fives. That's good. You have to have at least three of all these up here in order to get a bonus. Now it's my turn.'

Rodney rolled the dice and I curled up in a ball, because I could feel someone passing by very close to me. It ran through me like a shock and I stared at the dice Rodney had thrown.

'I'm collecting twos. Watch now, Anna.'

I watched as he rolled again and he got three more twos.

'Yahtzee,' said Rodney. 'I got really lucky there,' he said, sounding apologetic. He probably wanted me to win, but I thought about the shock that had gone through me, which I could still feel like a mix between a blow and a caress.

'Rodney, can we stop now?'

'Yes,' said Rodney. 'It was good that you tried. Next time we'll play longer.'

I nodded and went into my room. Sara was there, and she was lying down and reading a magazine, but I didn't care. She wasn't a danger to me. We weren't alike. I was sure of that, and the bed received me and I crept under the blanket and the sheet and it was like half of me was asleep and half of me was wide awake. I tried to put the awake side to sleep, the side that wandered out into the ward looking for something. I saw Rodney sitting in the common room, and Nurse Inga handing out medicine. And then the line of patients outside the nurses' office. Who was there? A girl with her hair up in a ponytail. Was it me? What was I doing there? And behind me in line, a man, and I turned around and looked into his face. It was Conrad. It was Conrad, standing there with his black hair and his eyes coloured by the sea and he looked at me and for one instant each of us saw who the other was.

'Anna,' he said. 'Anna, are you here?'

'Yes,' I said. 'I'm here.'

I took his hand. It was dry and warm and it closed around mine. Conrad's hand. My father. It was my father, standing in front of me and holding my hand. It wasn't frightening like everything else. Had he been there all along? I looked and looked into his eyes, which told me that I was lost and found. I wanted to say something more to him, something important, but I was back in my bed and all alone. What had happened? The giant's foot pressed into me and I sank into bed and Inga who came in with the medicine shouted my name. Why was she shouting? I got the IV and that meant I would end up in the soft place without colours and I took them and asked for more and the moment was over and Conrad had never been there.

Inga moved on to Sara, who was crying,

and Inga sat down with her for a moment and I died there, in bed, and no one noticed it, how the darkness threw itself over me. I said some sort of farewell and if I were ever to wake up again I would be in a completely different place.

THE LIGHT. THE white light hitting us. And the scents: dirt and something sweet was there behind it, blending together. We walked across the dry mountains and listened to the crickets. Conrad's hand was dry and soft, and he held me just like I held him. We walked on the path, and the sky was round as a ball with the sea down there.

'The sea,' said Conrad. 'That's the sea, Anna.'

'Yes,' I said. 'That's the sea.'

Because I could see. I saw the blue-green down there, stretching all the way to the horizon. We walked and it was like we were walking in heaven, because the clouds were below us. *Now I've seen the sea*, I thought. *Now it can all end.* We were so small beside the sea. Destroyed, without knowing it. The mild breeze stroked my cheek, pulled gently at my clothes. We climbed down, grabbing onto small bushes so we wouldn't fall.

Down, down to the sea that glittered. Then a roar behind us: an airplane breaking away and climbing, just behind us. I could almost reach up and touch it. I followed the plane's path across the sky, the white line it was writing on the sky.

'They're going to die,' said Conrad, and I nodded.

I could already see it before me. The dead hanging in their seats as the plane travelled on through the sky. The dead pilots and the cargo of gods that had come to fetch us.

'But we're already here,' I whispered. 'We are already here.'

Conrad, climbing down there. I had to get to him. I wanted my distance to him to be as short as possible, so I put one foot behind the other and pulled leaves from the bushes and the strong scent of the bushes hit me. Down there: a small rocky beach. We were heading for it. I slipped and slid down, cutting my knee, but I didn't care about the blood; I only saw Conrad and the sea down there.

The beach unfolded. I took off my clothes. I walked straight in and took my first stroke. And then another. My body stretched out with my strokes and I could feel the water all around me, like a caress. The water seemed both to hold me and to push me on. I heard Conrad behind me. He was swimming too. I saw a point out there, where the sea met the sky, and that's where I was going. I was happy? Certainly that's what I was, with my body just stretching out in stroke after stroke. I was happy with Conrad there behind me. So terribly happy.

RACHEL WILLSON-BROYLES is a freelance translator based in Saint Paul, Minnesota. She received her BA in Scandinavian Studies from Gustavus Adolphus College in 2002 and her PhD in Scandinavian Studies from the University of Wisconsin-Madison in 2013. Other authors whose works she has translated include Jonas Hassen Khemiri, Jonas Jonasson, and Malin Persson Giolito.

On the Design

As book design is an integral part of the reading experience, we would like to acknowledge the work of those who shaped the form in which the story is housed.

Tessa van der Waals (Netherlands) is responsible for the cover design, cover typography, and art direction of all World Editions books. She works in the internationally renowned tradition of Dutch Design. Her bright and powerful visual aesthetic maintains a harmony between image and typography and captures the unique atmosphere of each book. She works closely with internationally celebrated photographers, artists, and letter designers. Her work has frequently been awarded prizes for Best Dutch Book Design.

Paul Citroen (1896–1983) was a Dutch artist and teacher who received his education at the Bauhaus in Weimar. His oeuvre includes paintings, photos, and stamp designs. His most famous work is perhaps "Metropolis" (1923), a photo montage of a large city that inspired the German director Fritz Lang in the making of the now classic film of the same name. The photograph on the cover is of his niece Eva Bendien, who was born in Arnhem in 1921 and later went on to become a gallery owner and art dealer.

The cover has been edited by lithographer Bert van der Horst of BFC Graphics (Netherlands).

Suzan Beijer (Netherlands) is responsible for the typography and careful interior book design of all World Editions titles.

The text on the inside covers and the press quotes are set in Circular, designed by Laurenz Brunner (Switzerland) and published by Swiss type foundry Lineto.

All World Editions books are set in the typeface Dolly, specifically designed for book typography. Dolly creates a warm page image perfect for an enjoyable reading experience. This typeface is designed by Underware, a European collective formed by Bas Jacobs (Netherlands), Akiem Helmling (Germany), and Sami Kortemäki (Finland). Underware are also the creators of the World Editions logo, which meets the design requirement that "a strong shape can always be drawn with a toe in the sand."